You know you want to read
ALL the Pizza and Taco books!

WHO'S THE BEST?

BEST PARTY EVER!

SUPER-AWESOME COMIC!

TOO COOL FOR SCHOOL

ROCK OUT!

DARE TO BE SCARED!

WRESTLING MANIA!
(Coming in January 2024)

Pizza and Taco

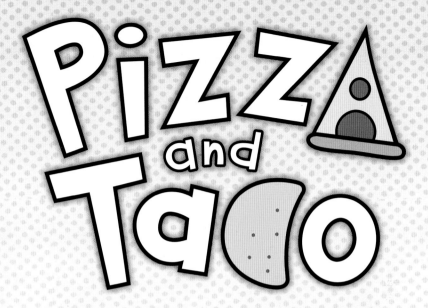

TOO COOL FOR SCHOOL

STEPHEN SHASKAN

WE are going to be the coolest kids in school.

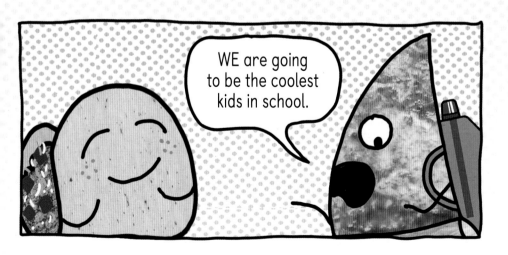

A STEPPING STONE BOOK™

Random House New York

To Finn and Stella, two cool kids

Copyright © 2022 by Stephen Shaskan
All rights reserved. Published in the United States by Random House Children's Books,
a division of Penguin Random House LLC, New York.
Random House and the colophon are registered trademarks and RH Graphic with
the book design is a trademark of Penguin Random House LLC.
Visit us on the Web! rhcbooks.com
Educators and librarians, for a variety of teaching tools, visit us at RHTeachersLibrarians.com

Library of Congress Cataloging-in-Publication Data is available upon request.
ISBN 978-0-593-37607-2 (trade) — ISBN 978-0-593-37608-9 (lib. bdg.) —
ISBN 978-0-593-37609-6 (ebook)

MANUFACTURED IN CHINA
10 9 8 7 6 5 4
First Edition

Contents

Chapter 1
Coolest Kids in School

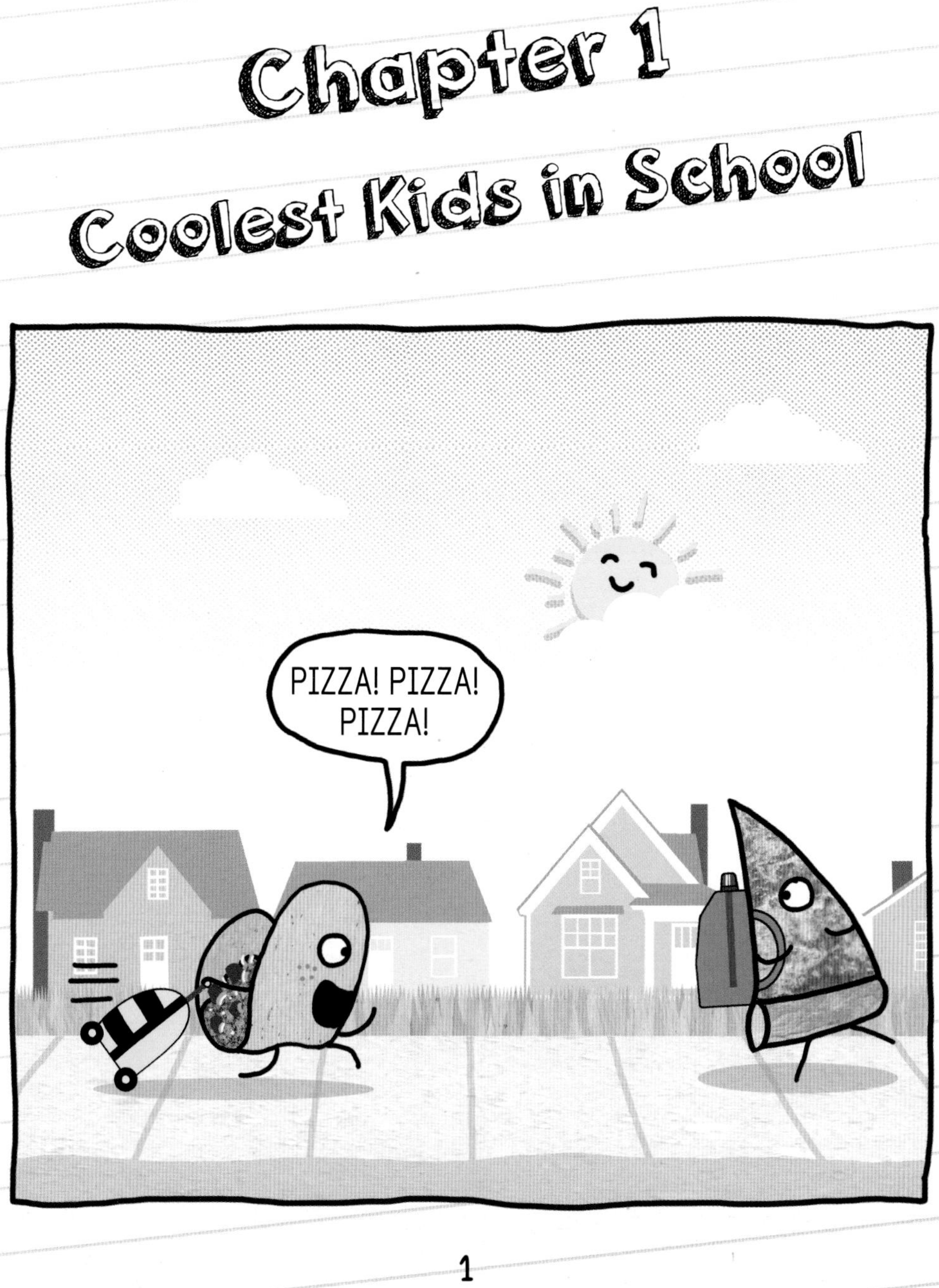
PIZZA! PIZZA! PIZZA!

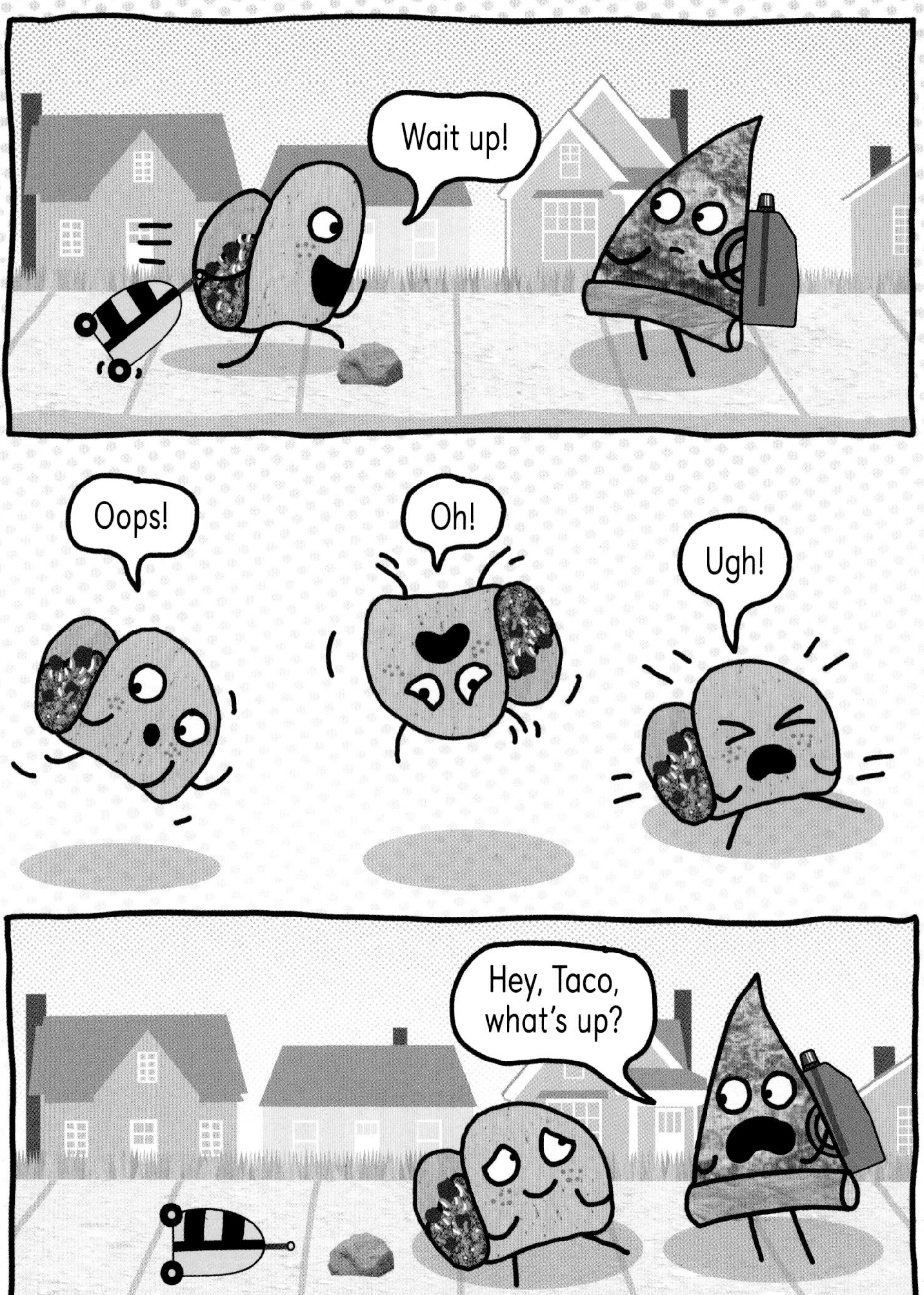
Wait up!
Oops!
Oh!
Ugh!
Hey, Taco, what's up?

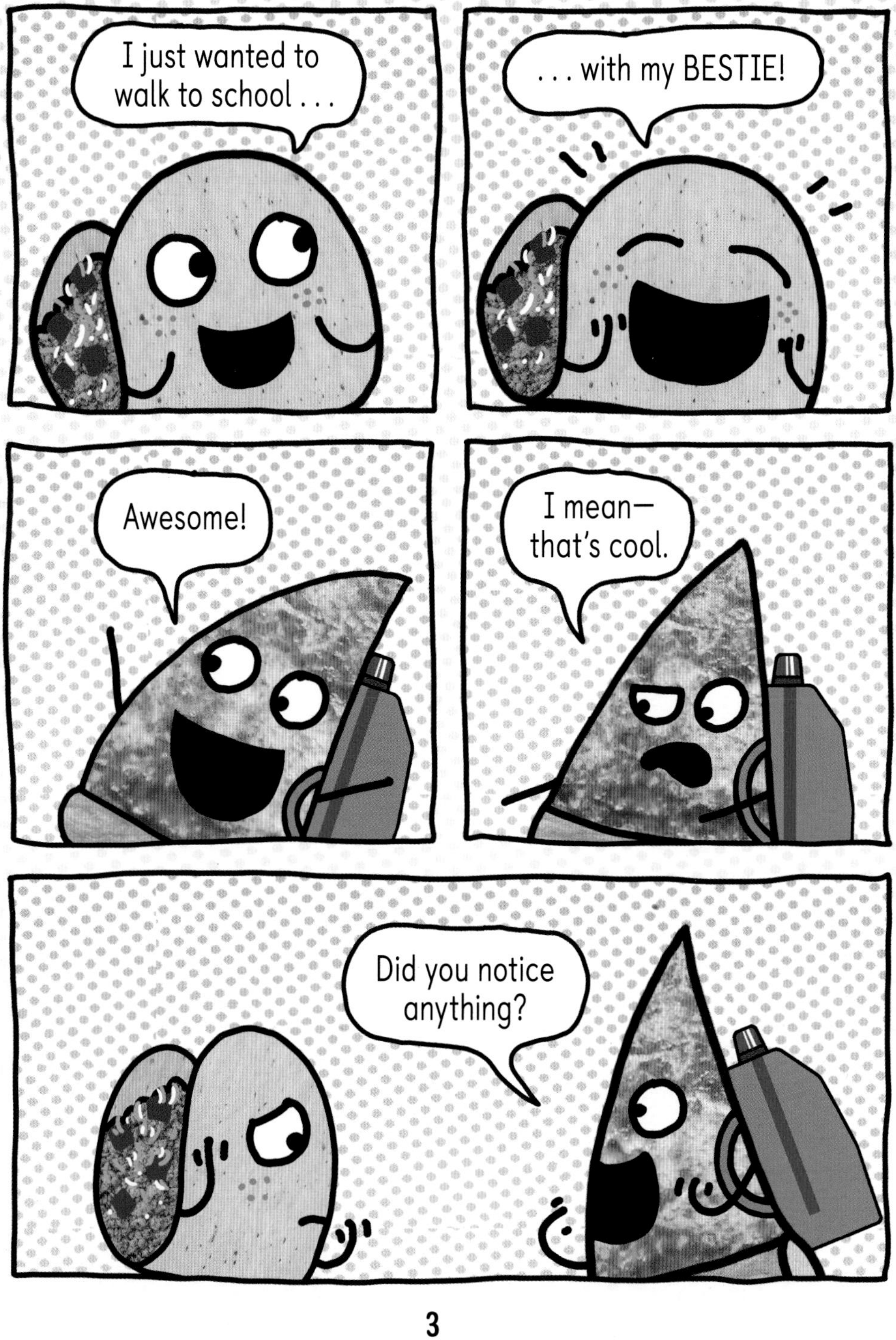
I just wanted to walk to school . . .
. . . with my BESTIE!
Awesome!
I mean— that's cool.
Did you notice anything?

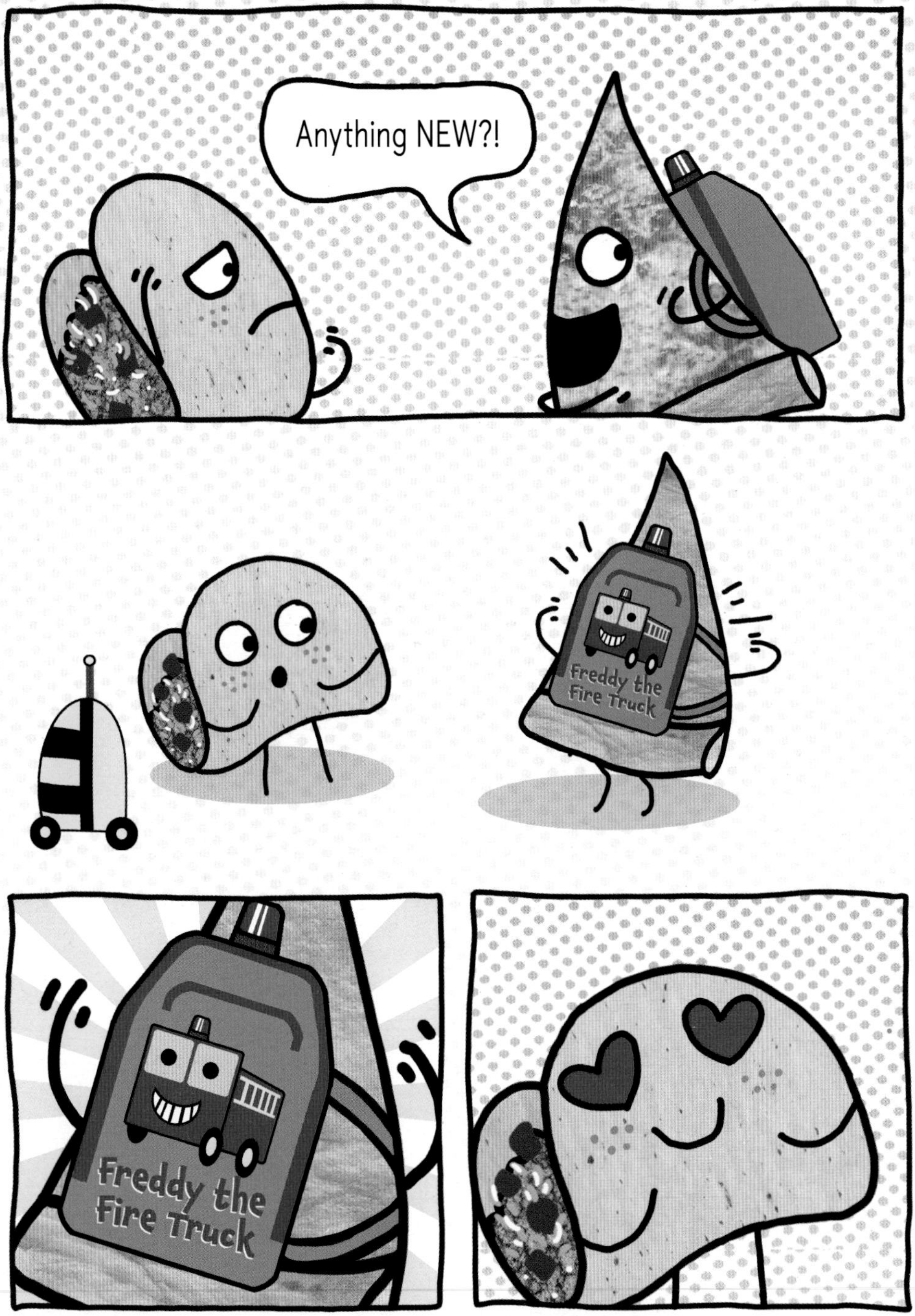
Anything NEW?!
Freddy the Fire Truck
Freddy the Fire Truck

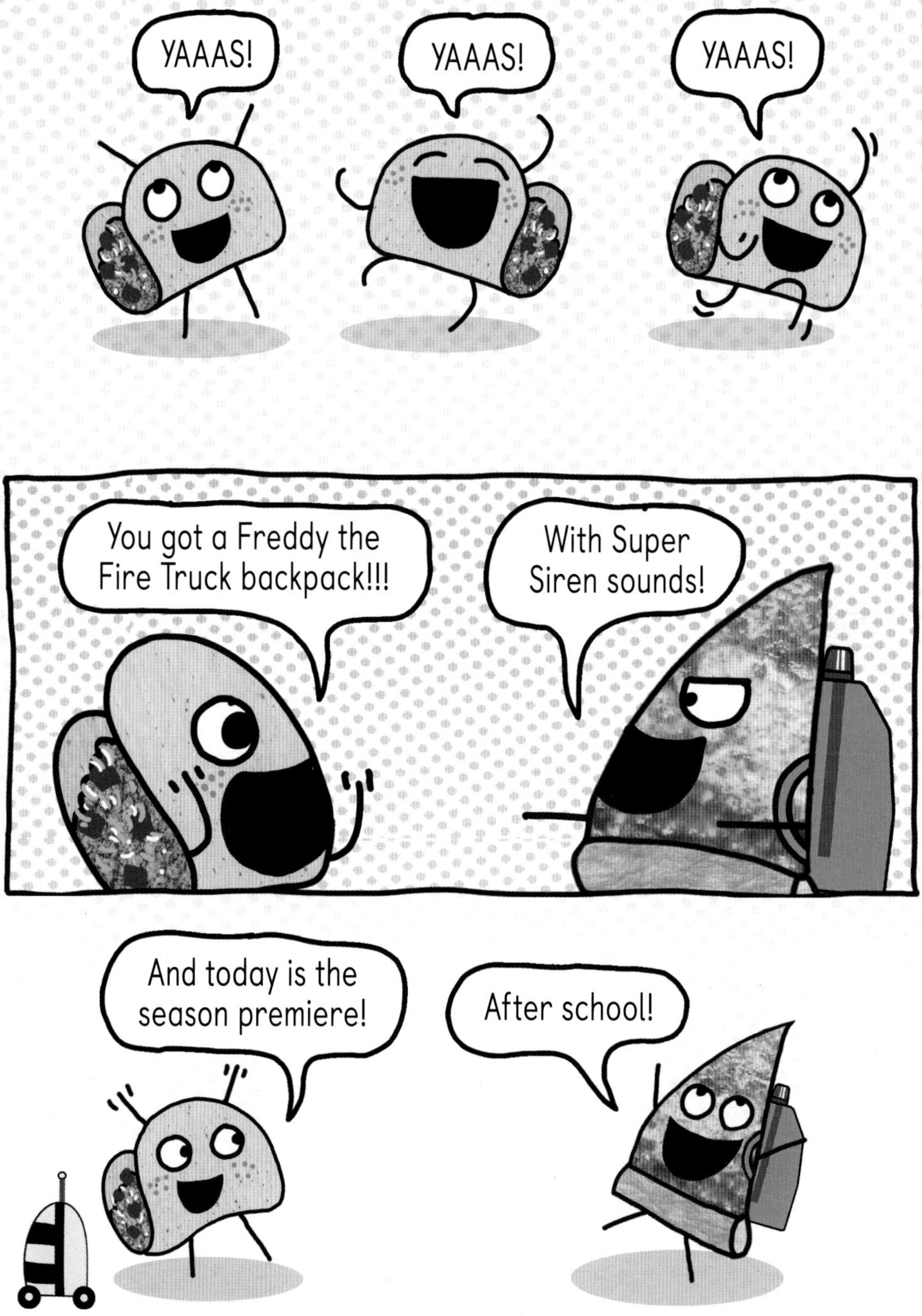
YAAAS!
YAAAS!
YAAAS!
You got a Freddy the Fire Truck backpack!!!
With Super Siren sounds!
And today is the season premiere!
After school!

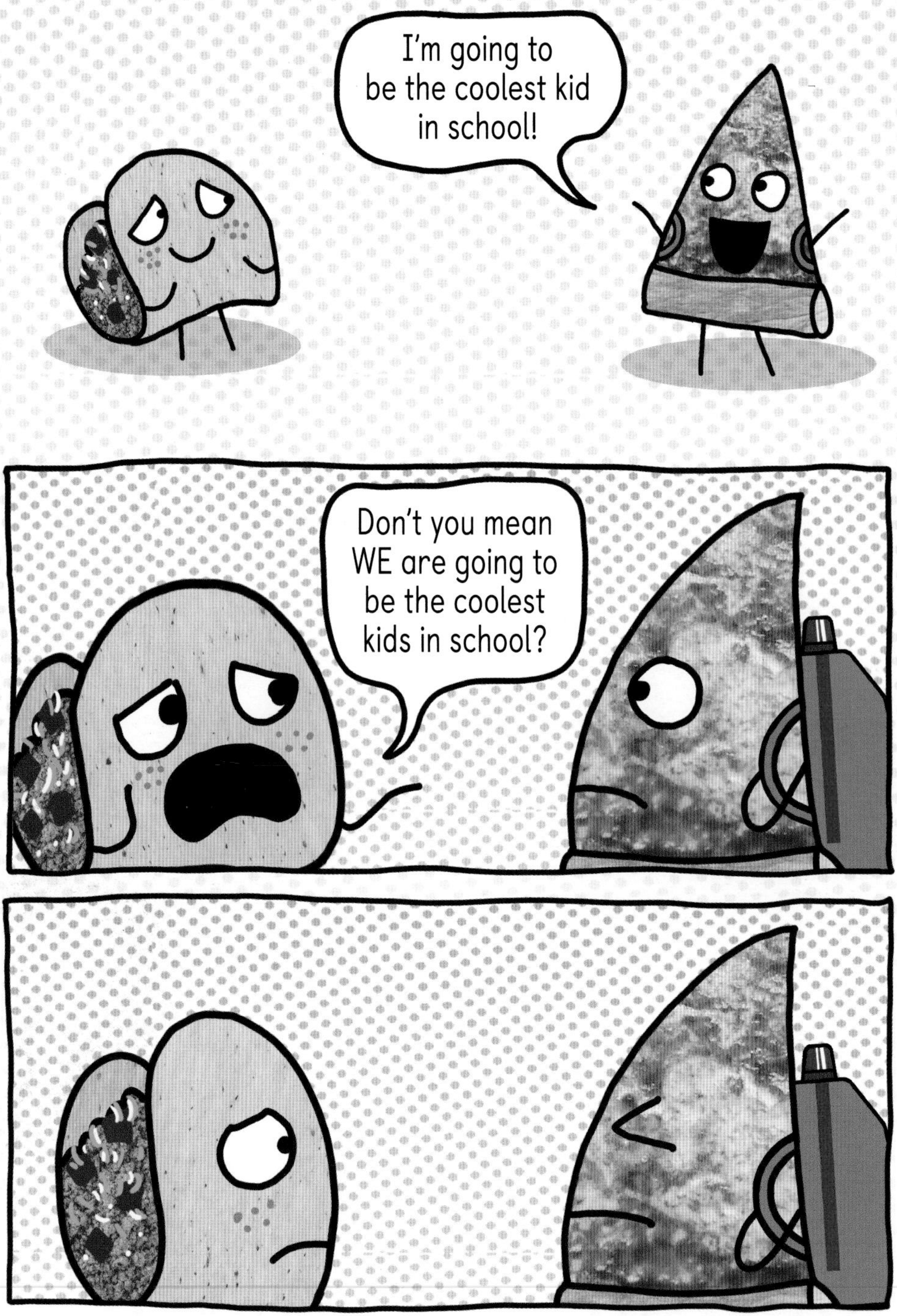
I'm going to be the coolest kid in school!
Don't you mean WE are going to be the coolest kids in school?

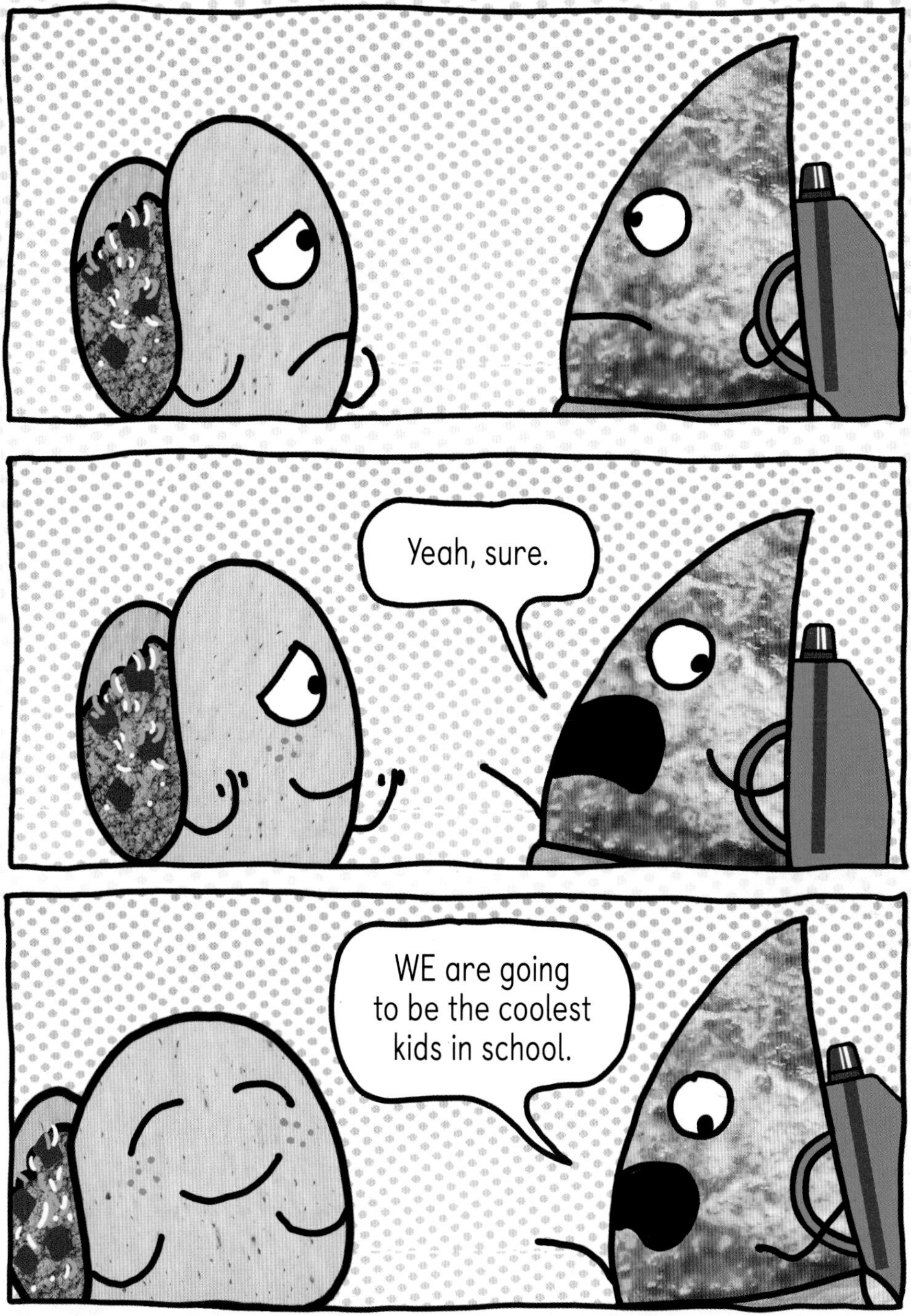
Yeah, sure.
WE are going to be the coolest kids in school.

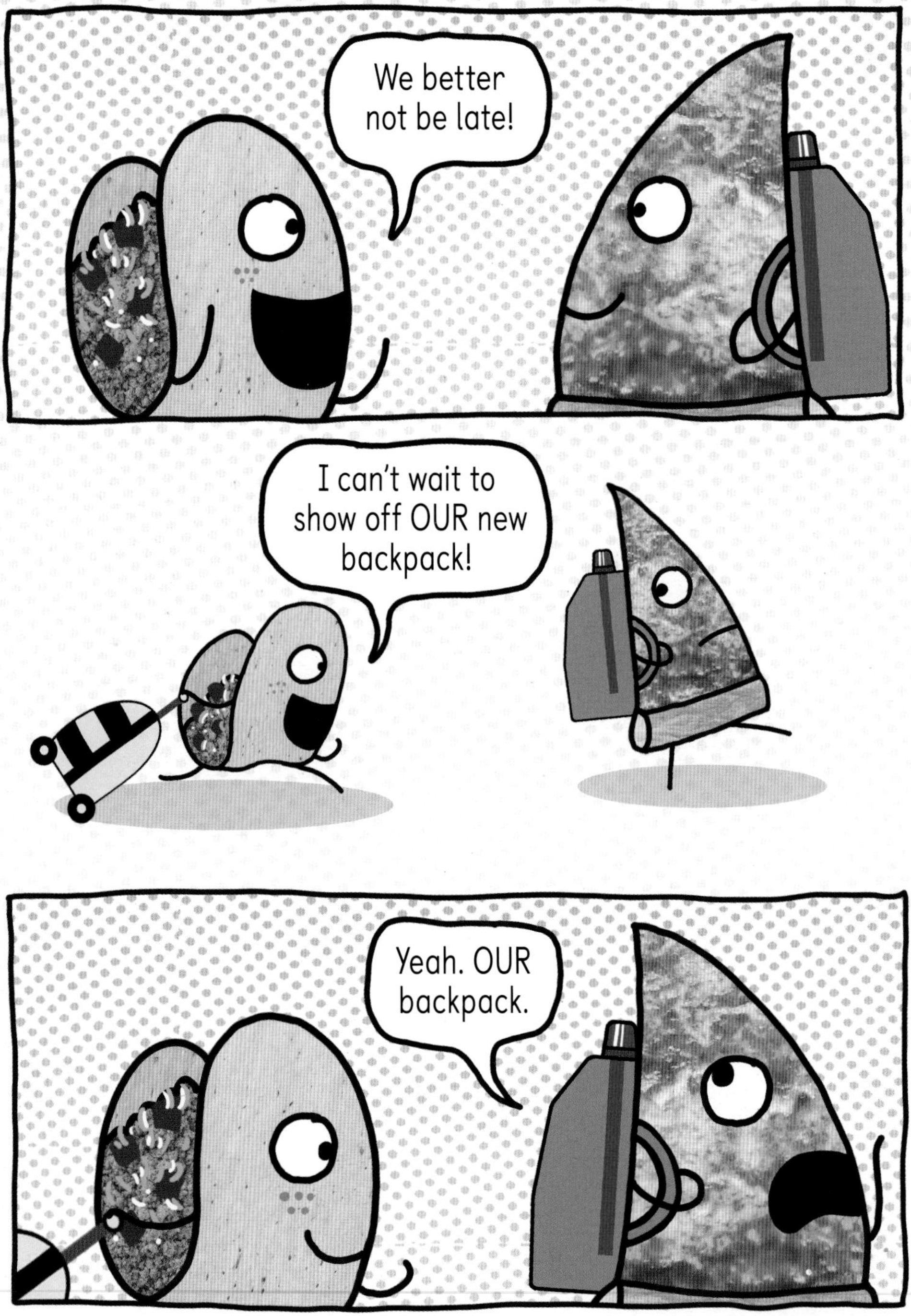
We better not be late!
I can't wait to show off OUR new backpack!
Yeah. OUR backpack.

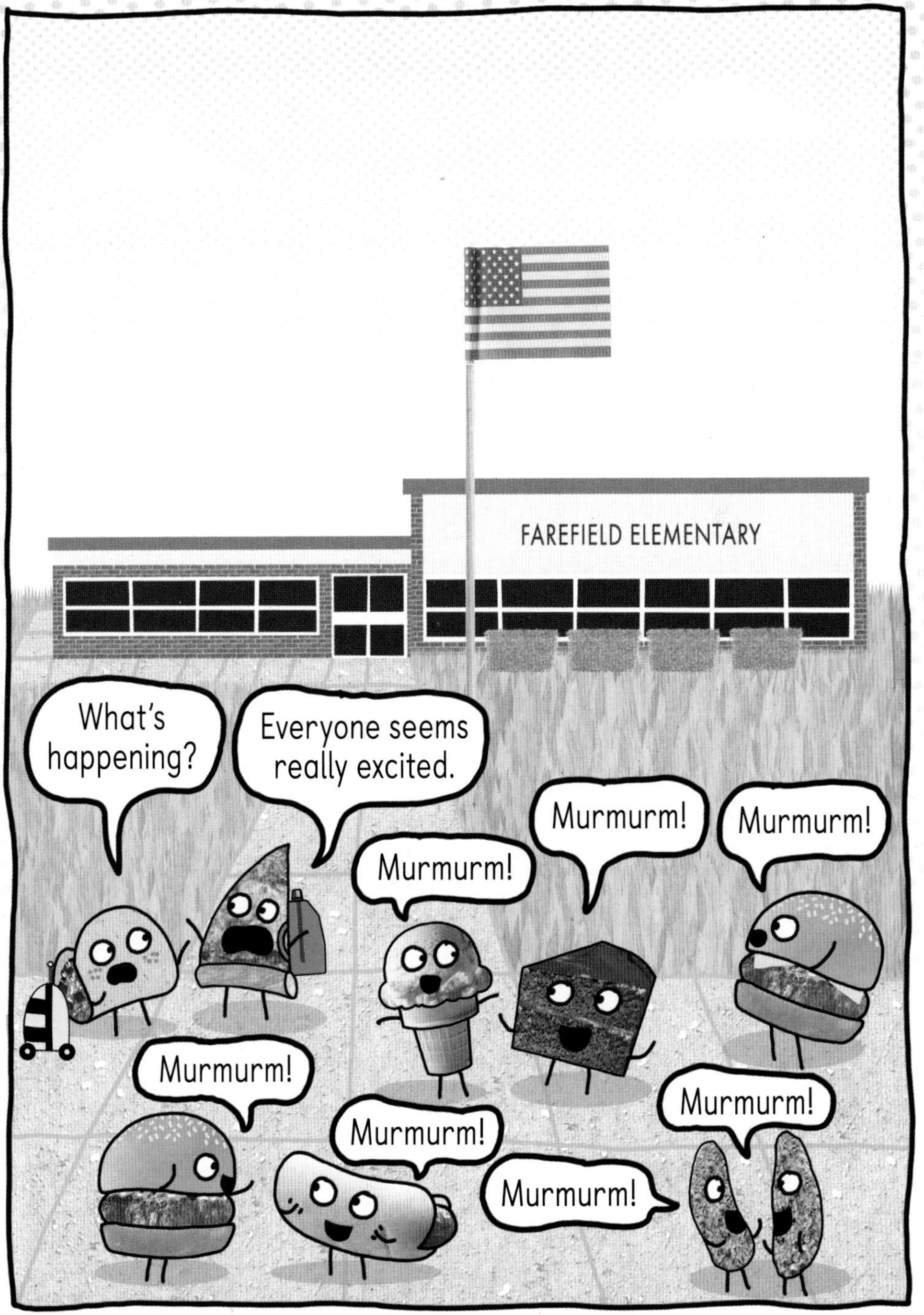
FAREFIELD ELEMENTARY
What's happening?
Everyone seems really excited.
Murmurm!
Murmurm!
Murmurm!
Murmurm!
Murmurm!
Murmurm!
Murmurm!

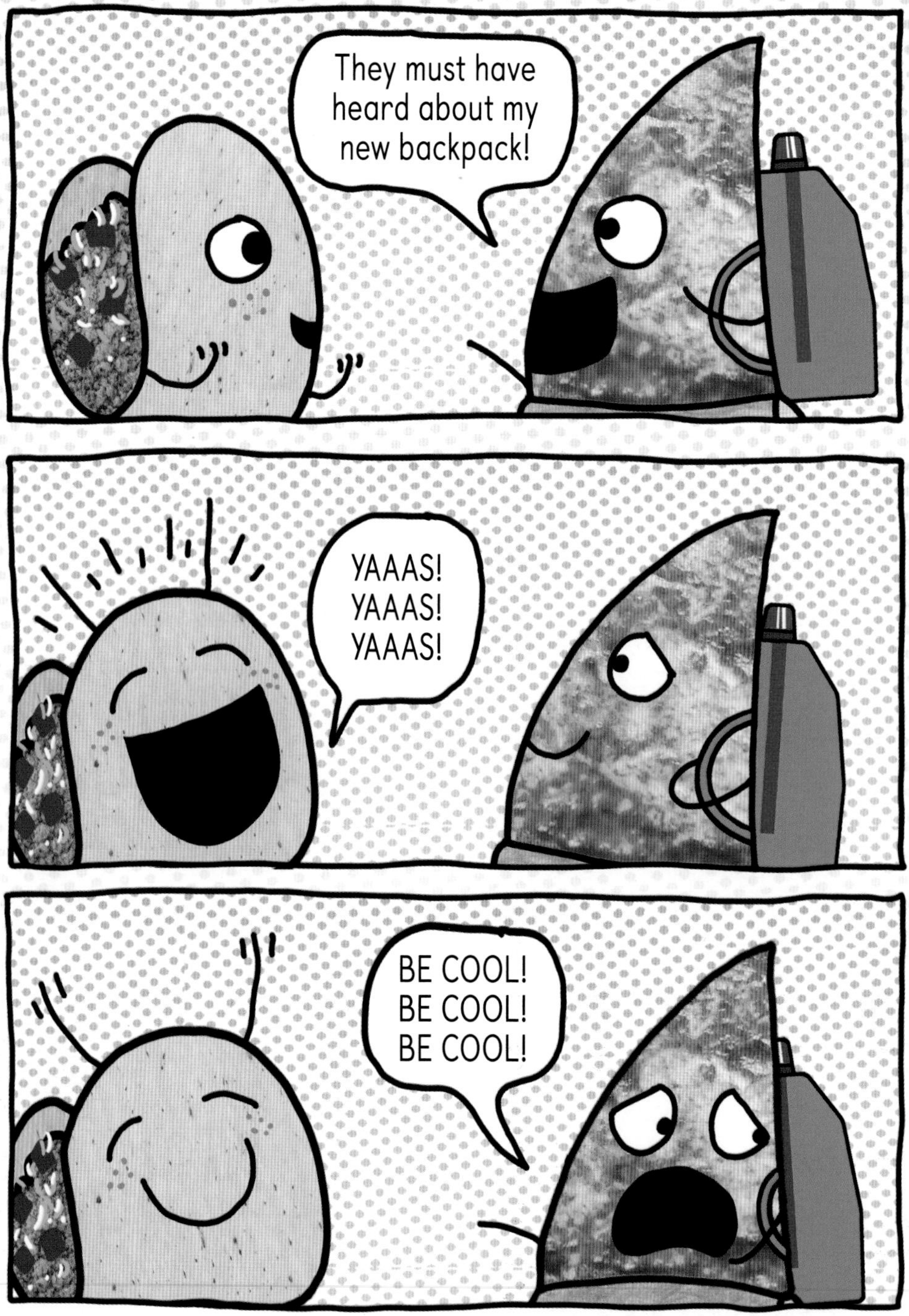
They must have heard about my new backpack!
YAAAS! YAAAS! YAAAS!
BE COOL! BE COOL! BE COOL!

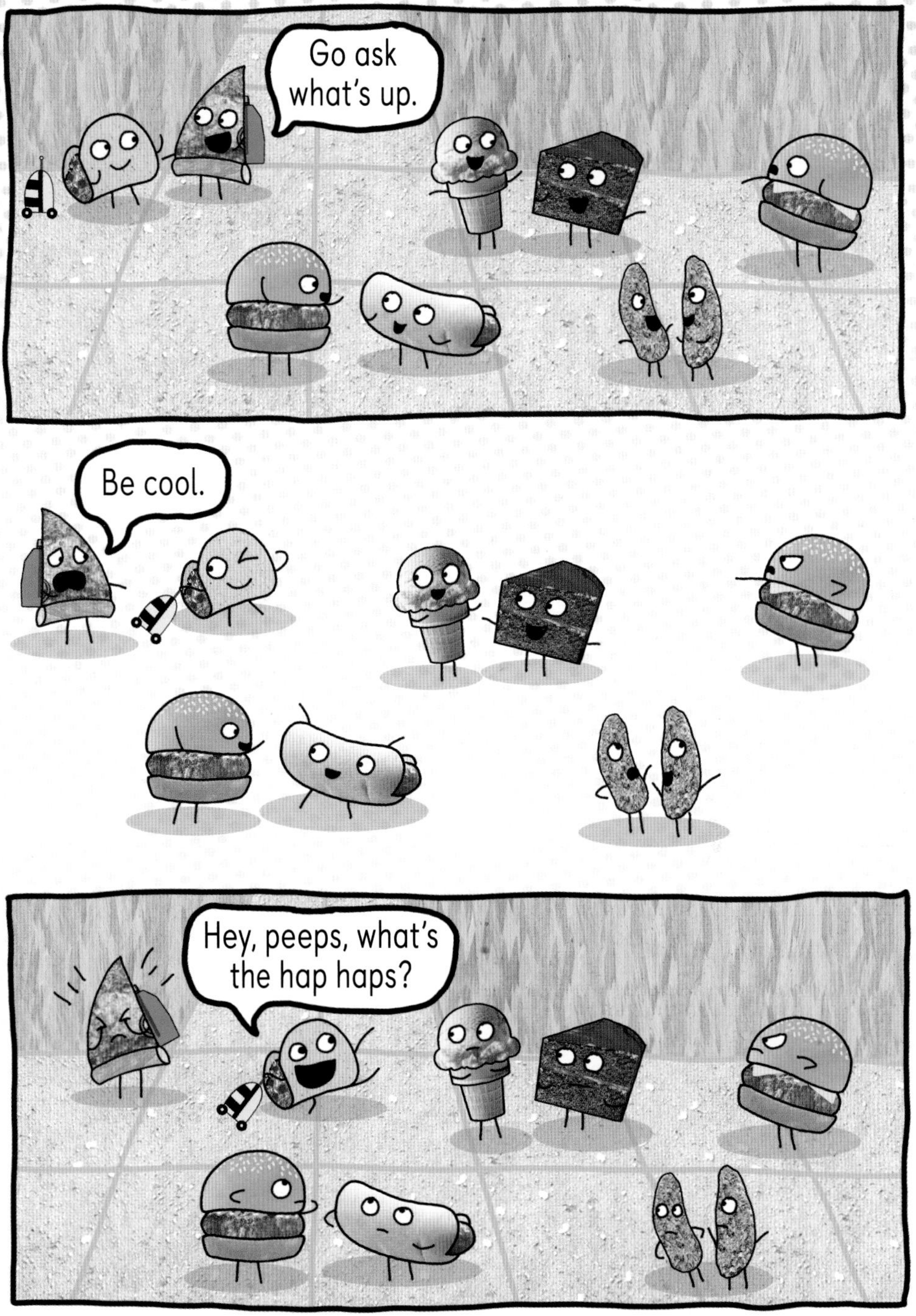
Go ask what's up.
Be cool.
Hey, peeps, what's the hap haps?

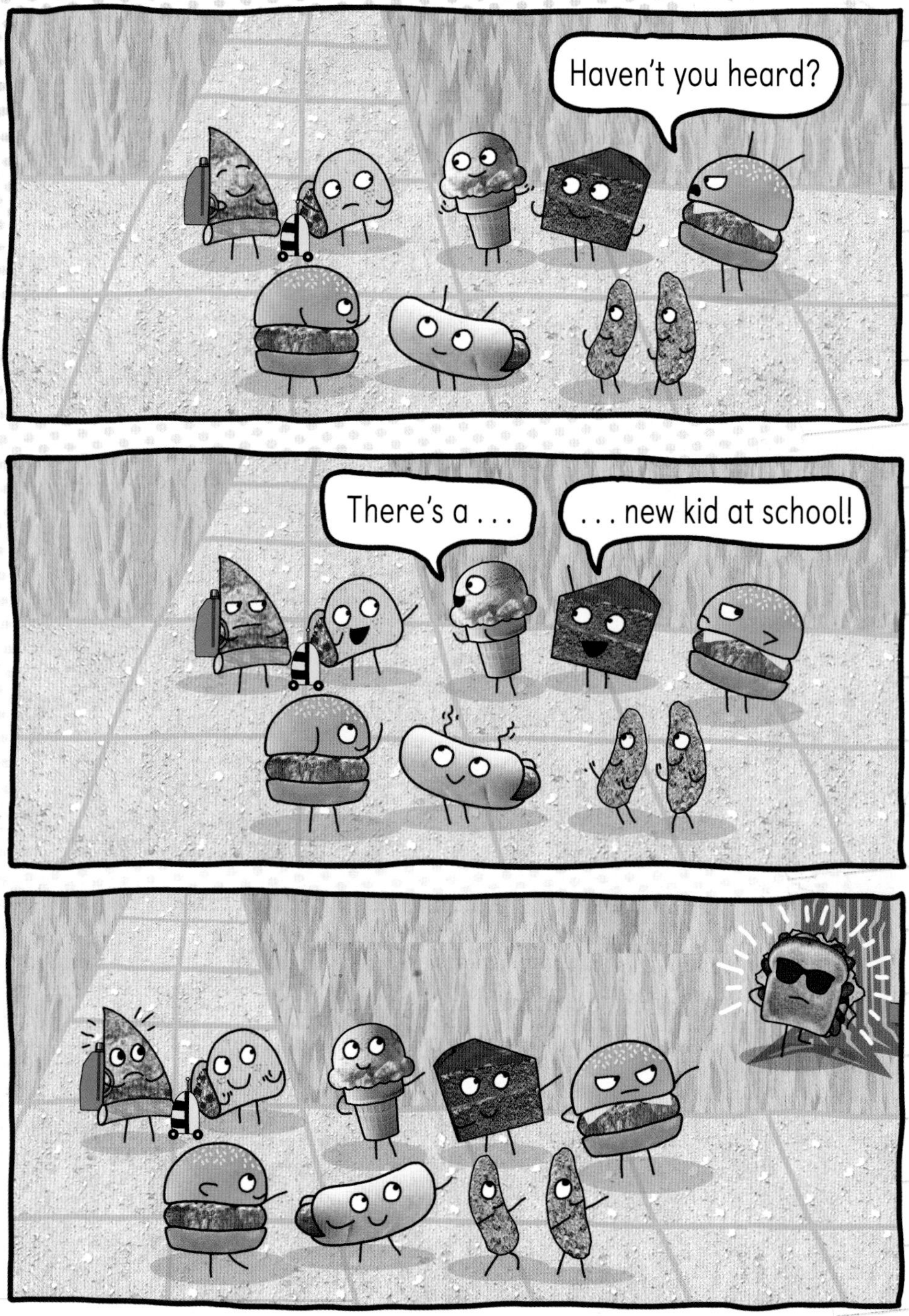
Haven't you heard?
There's a . . .
. . . new kid at school!

Chapter 2
The New Kid

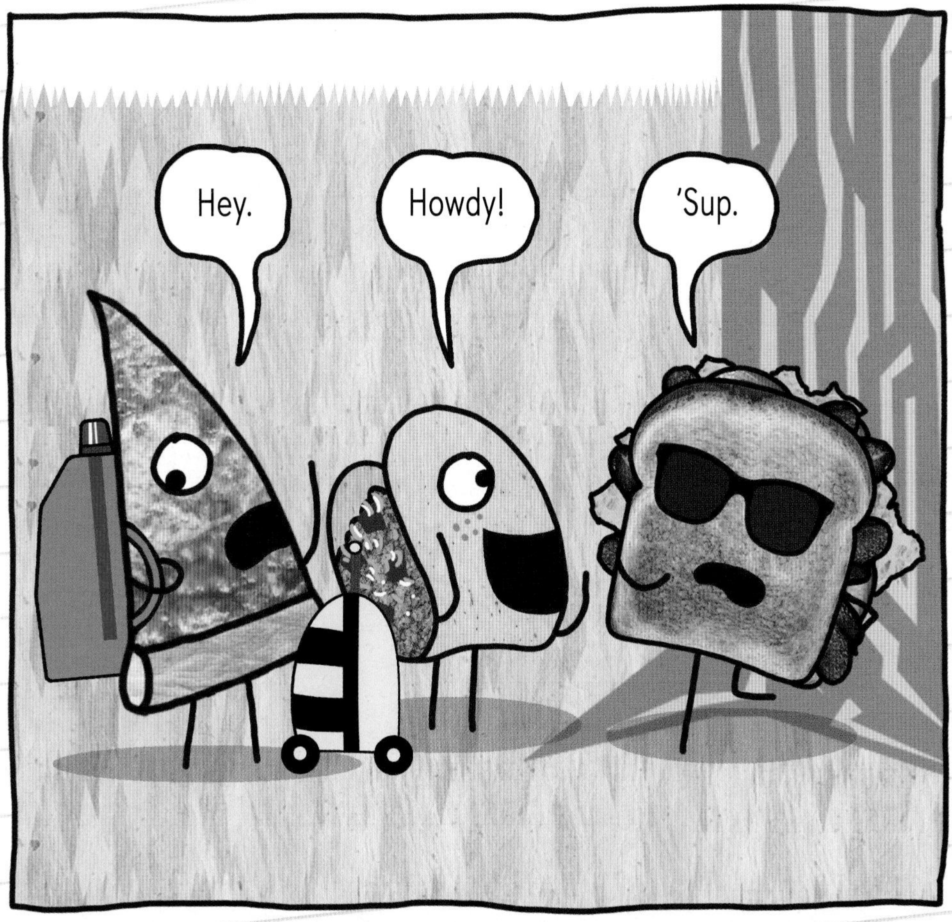
Hey.
Howdy!
'Sup.

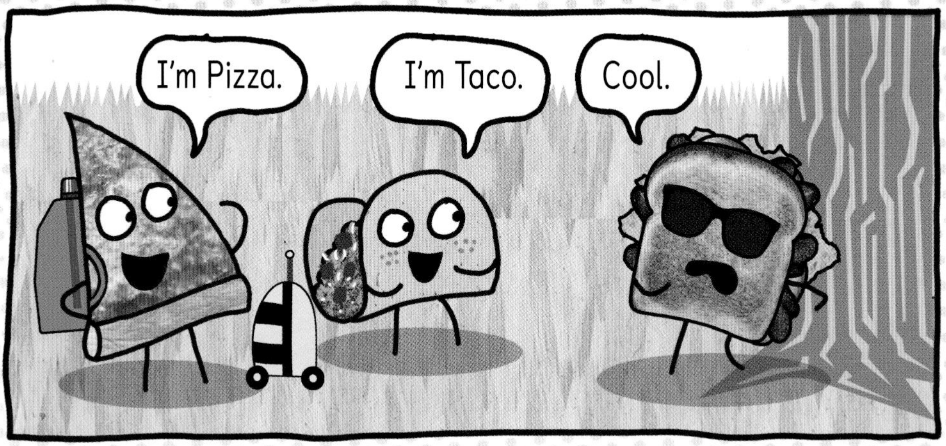
I'm Pizza.
I'm Taco.
Cool.

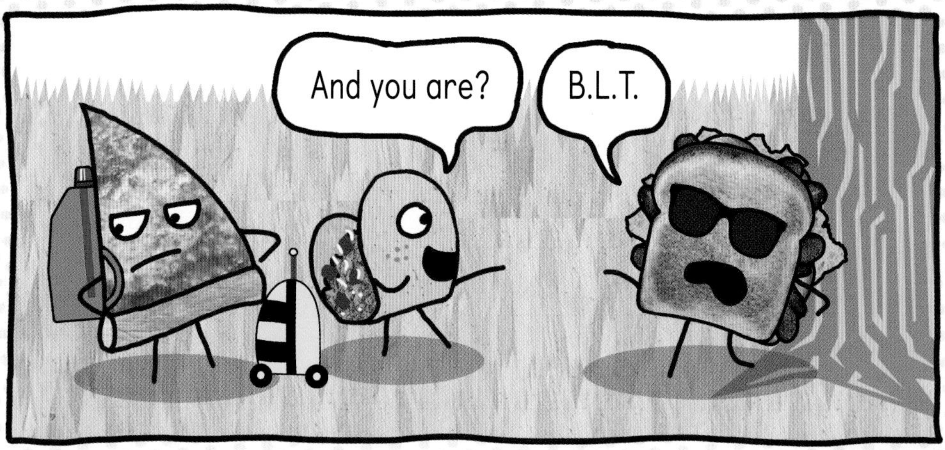
And you are?
B.L.T.

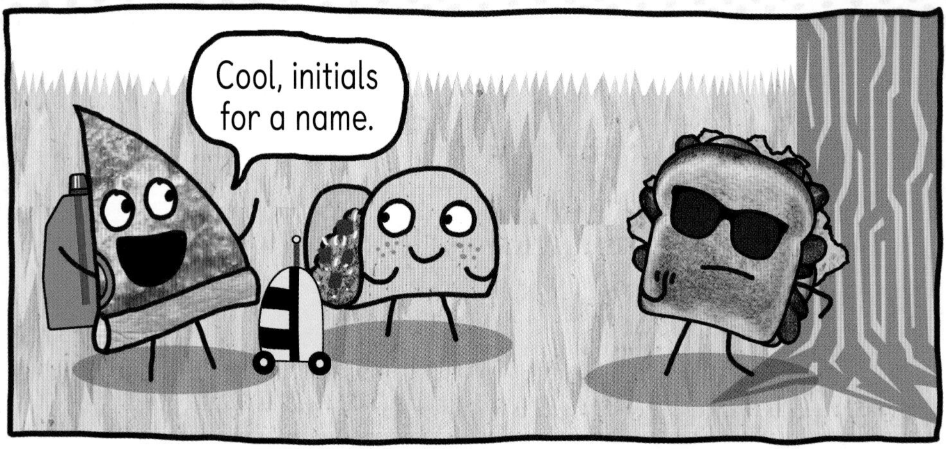
Cool, initials for a name.

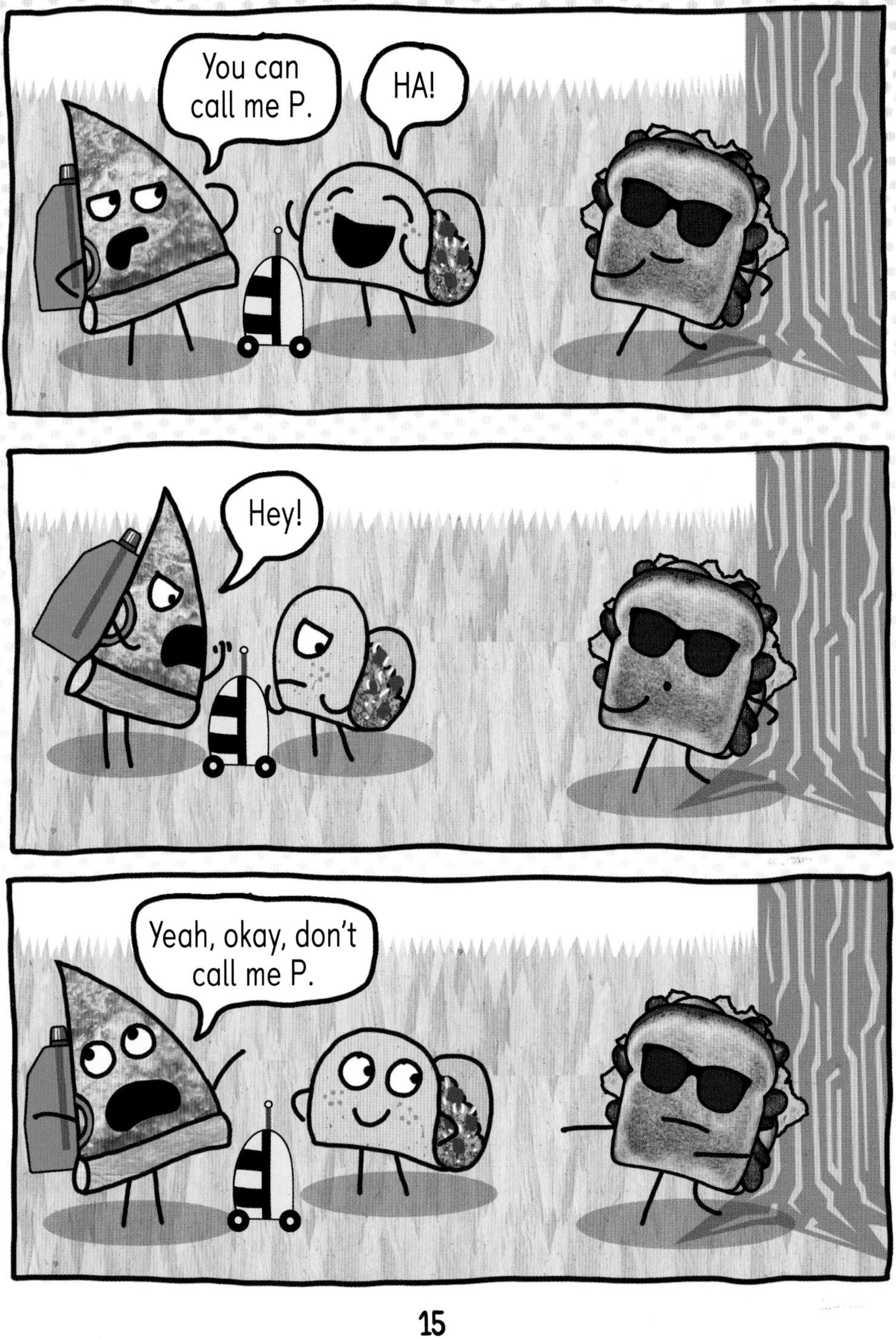
You can call me P.
HA!
Hey!
Yeah, okay, don't call me P.

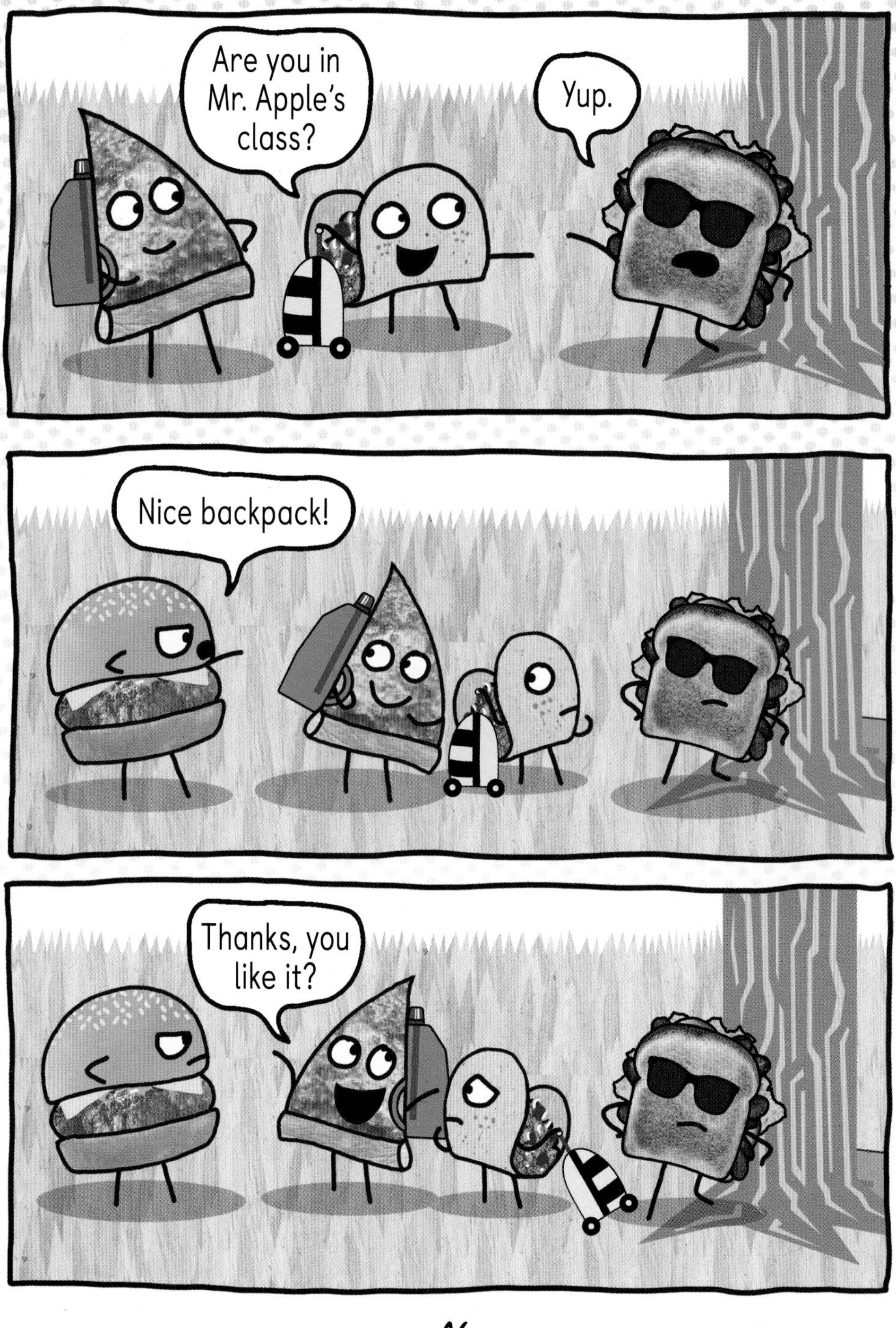
Are you in Mr. Apple's class?
Yup.
Nice backpack!
Thanks, you like it?

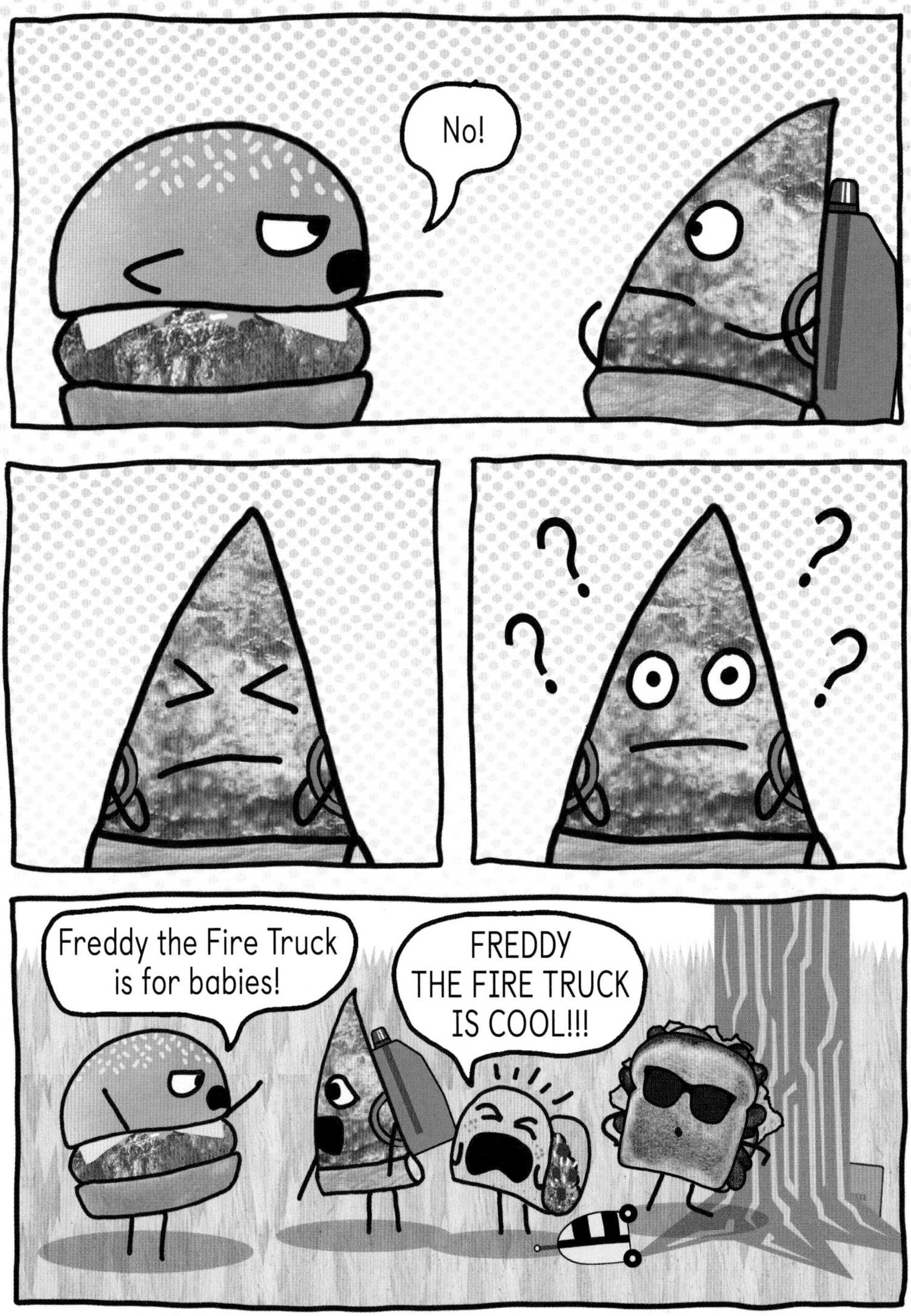
No!
Freddy the Fire Truck is for babies!
FREDDY THE FIRE TRUCK IS COOL!!!

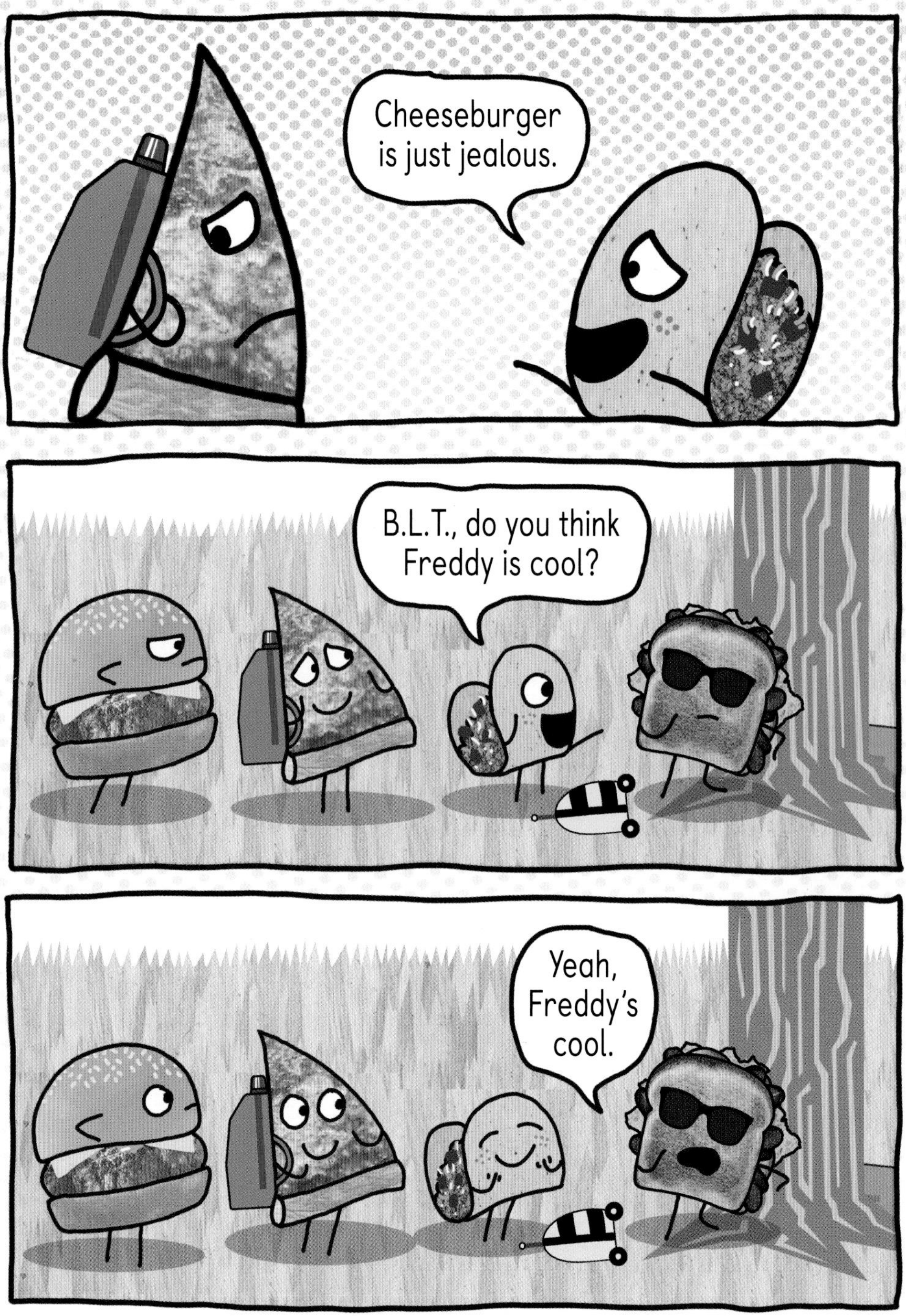
Cheeseburger is just jealous.
B.L.T., do you think Freddy is cool?
Yeah, Freddy's cool.

B.L.T. thinks Freddy's cool.
My baby cousin loves that show.

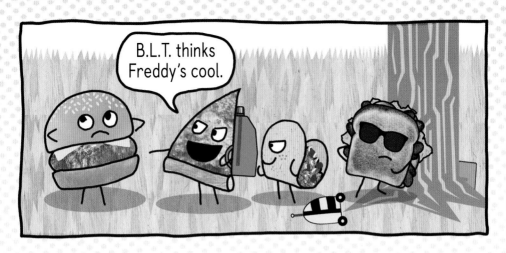

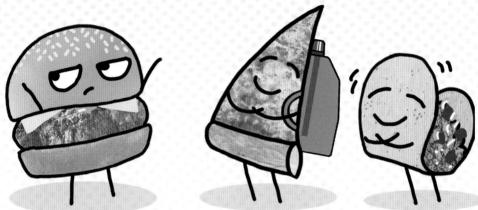

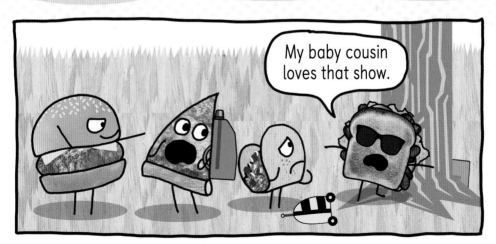

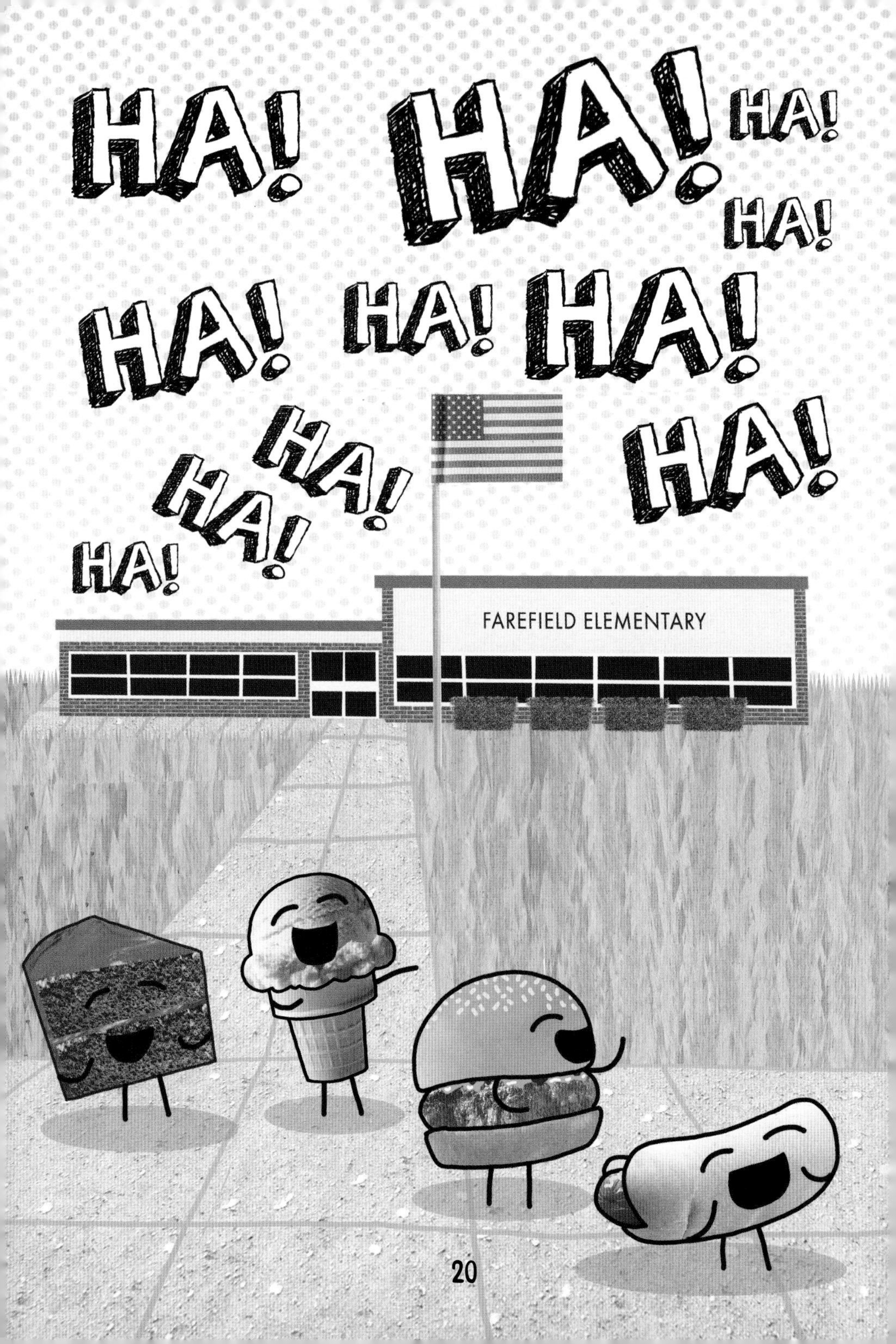
HA! HA! HA!
HA!
HA! HA! HA!
HA! HA!
HA! HA!
HA!
FAREFIELD ELEMENTARY

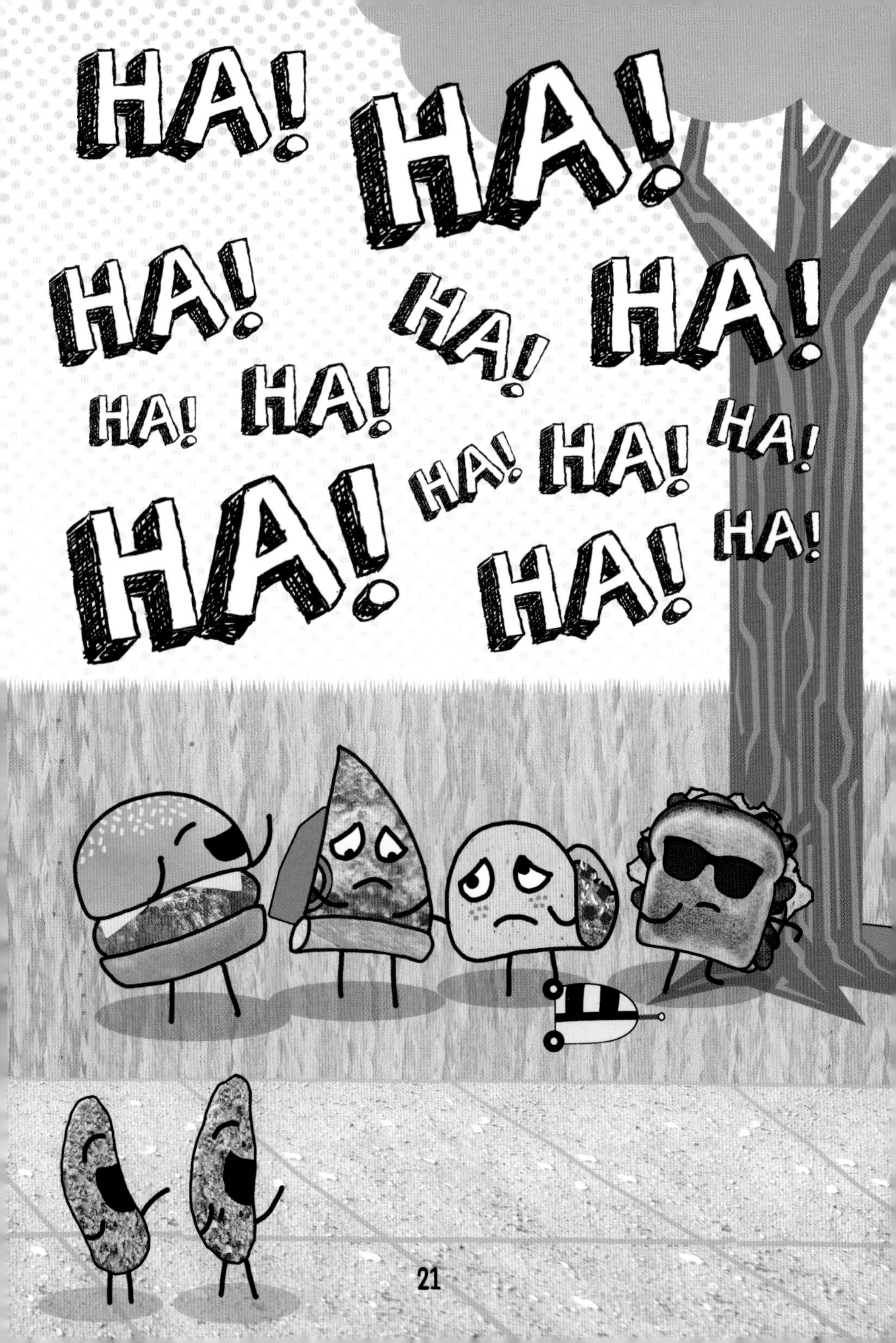
HA!
HA!
HA!
HA!
HA!
HA!
HA!
HA!
HA!
HA!
HA!
HA!
HA!

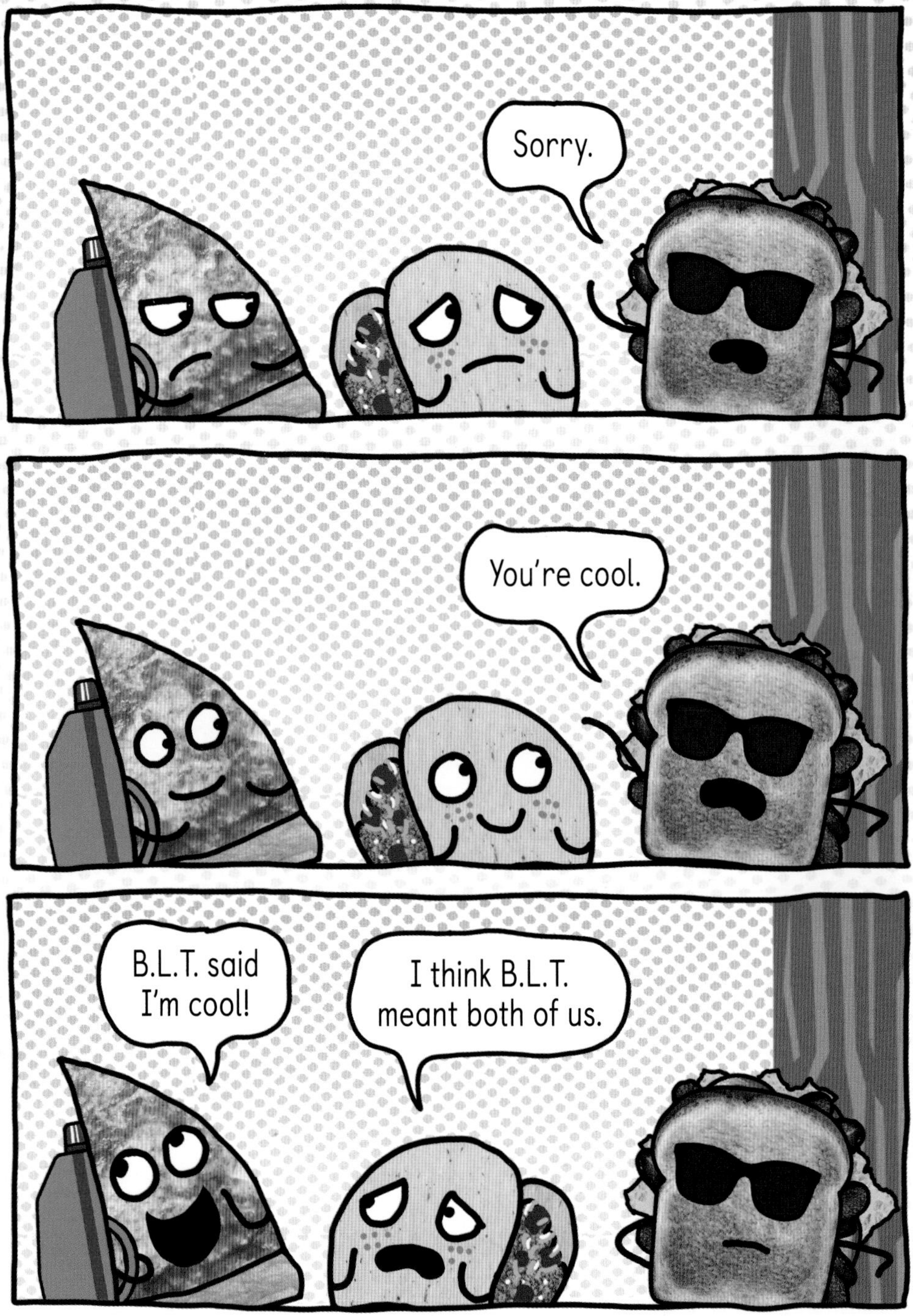
Sorry.
You're cool.
B.L.T. said I'm cool!
I think B.L.T. meant both of us.

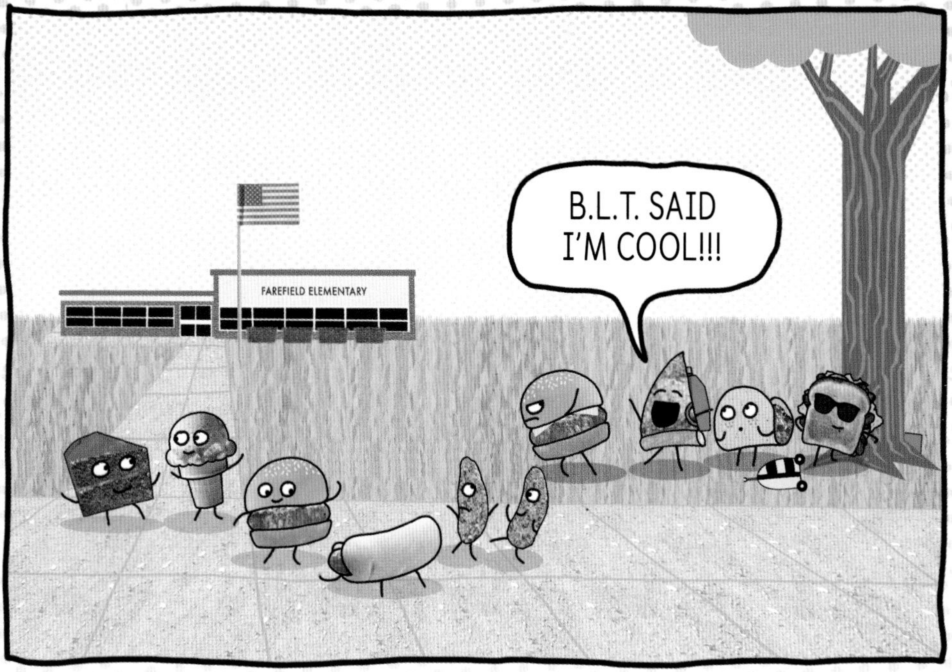
FAREFIELD ELEMENTARY
B.L.T. SAID
I'M COOL!!!

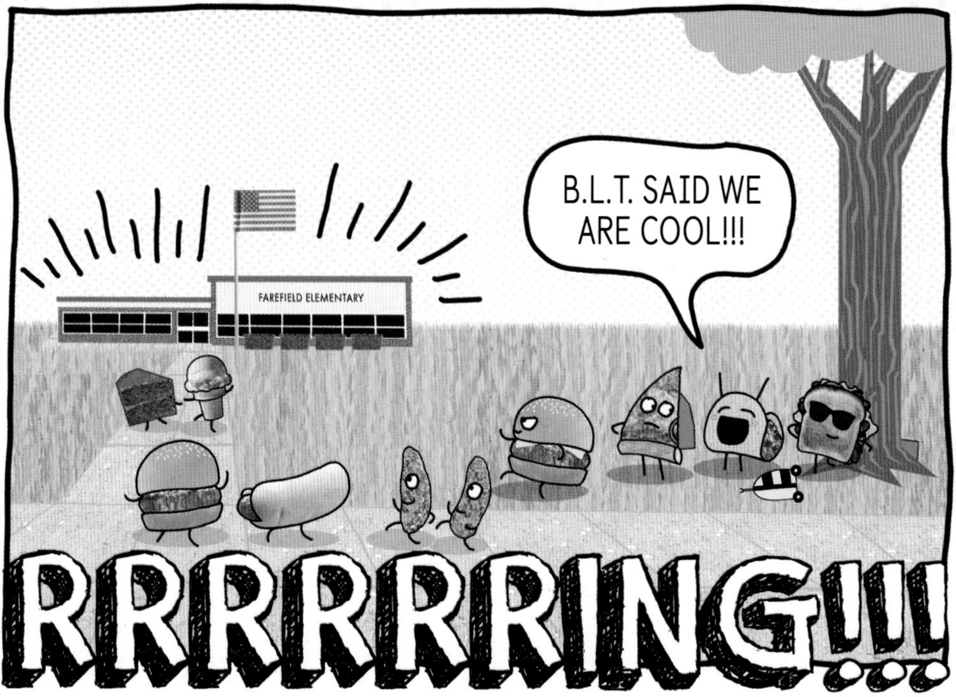
FAREFIELD ELEMENTARY
B.L.T. SAID WE
ARE COOL!!!
RRRRRRING!!!

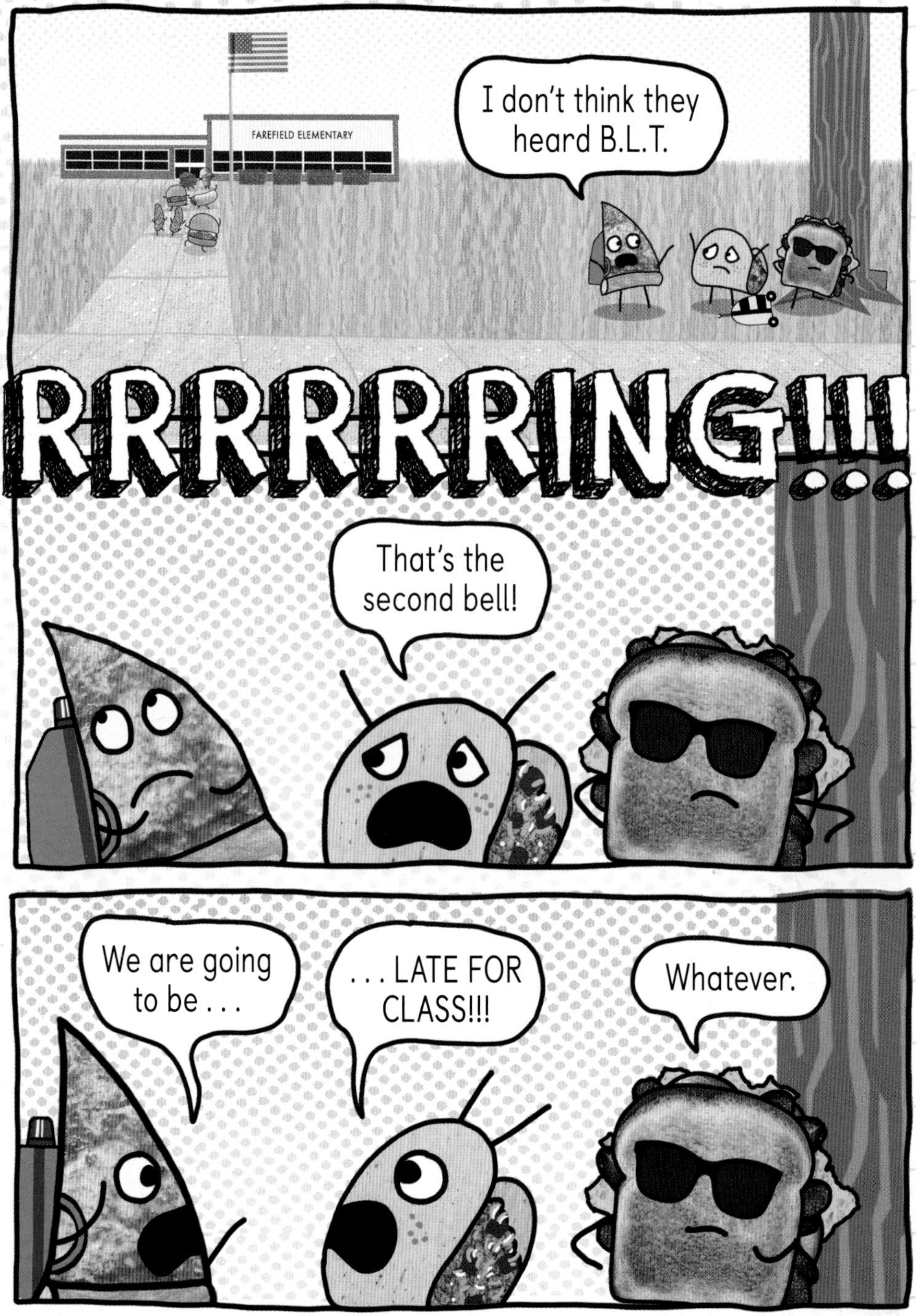
FAREFIELD ELEMENTARY
I don't think they heard B.L.T.
RRRRRRRING!!!
That's the second bell!
We are going to be . . .
. . . LATE FOR CLASS!!!
Whatever.

Chapter 3
Late for Class

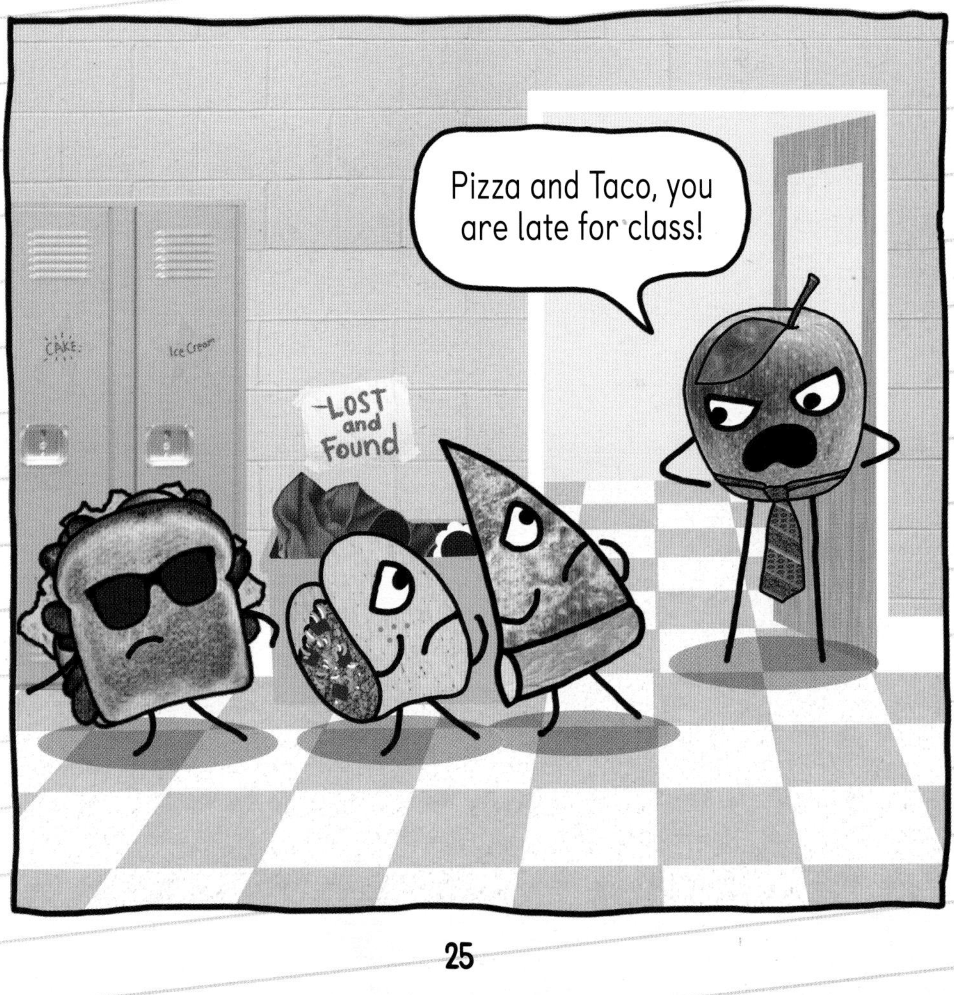

Pizza and Taco, you are late for class!
CAKE
Ice Cream
LOST and Found

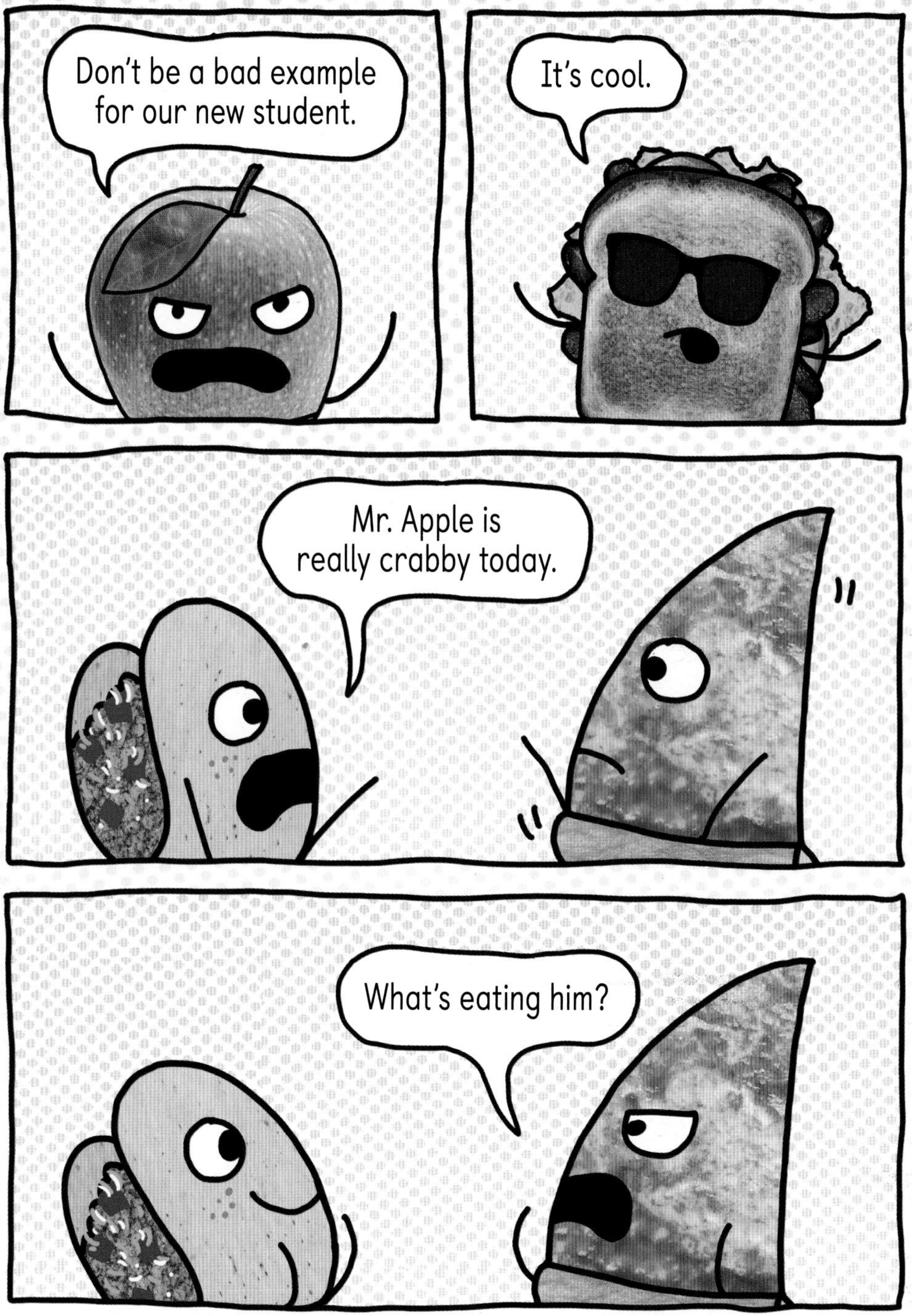
Don't be a bad example for our new student.
It's cool.
Mr. Apple is really crabby today.
What's eating him?

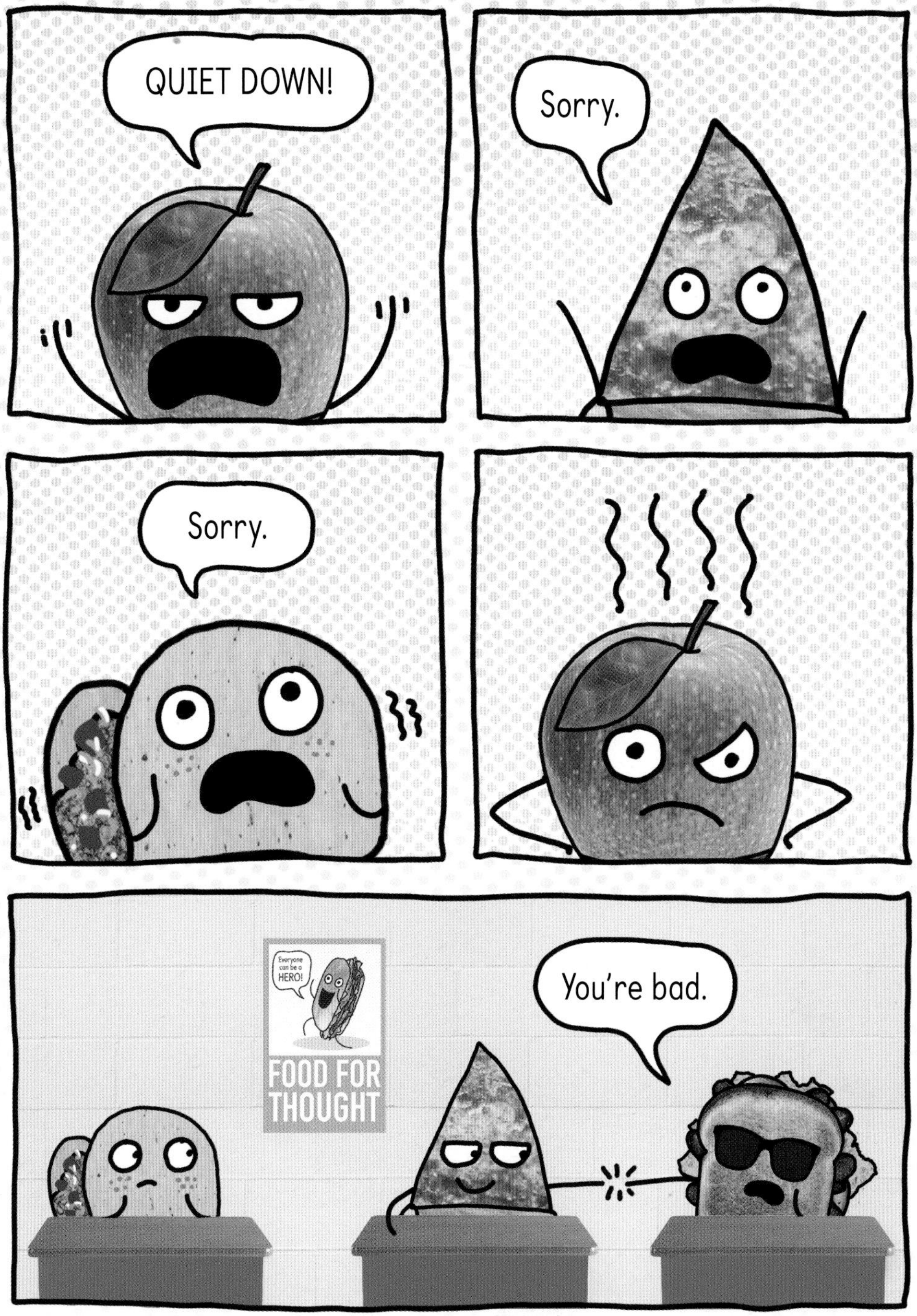
QUIET DOWN!
Sorry.
Sorry.
Everyone can be a HERO!
FOOD FOR THOUGHT
You're bad.

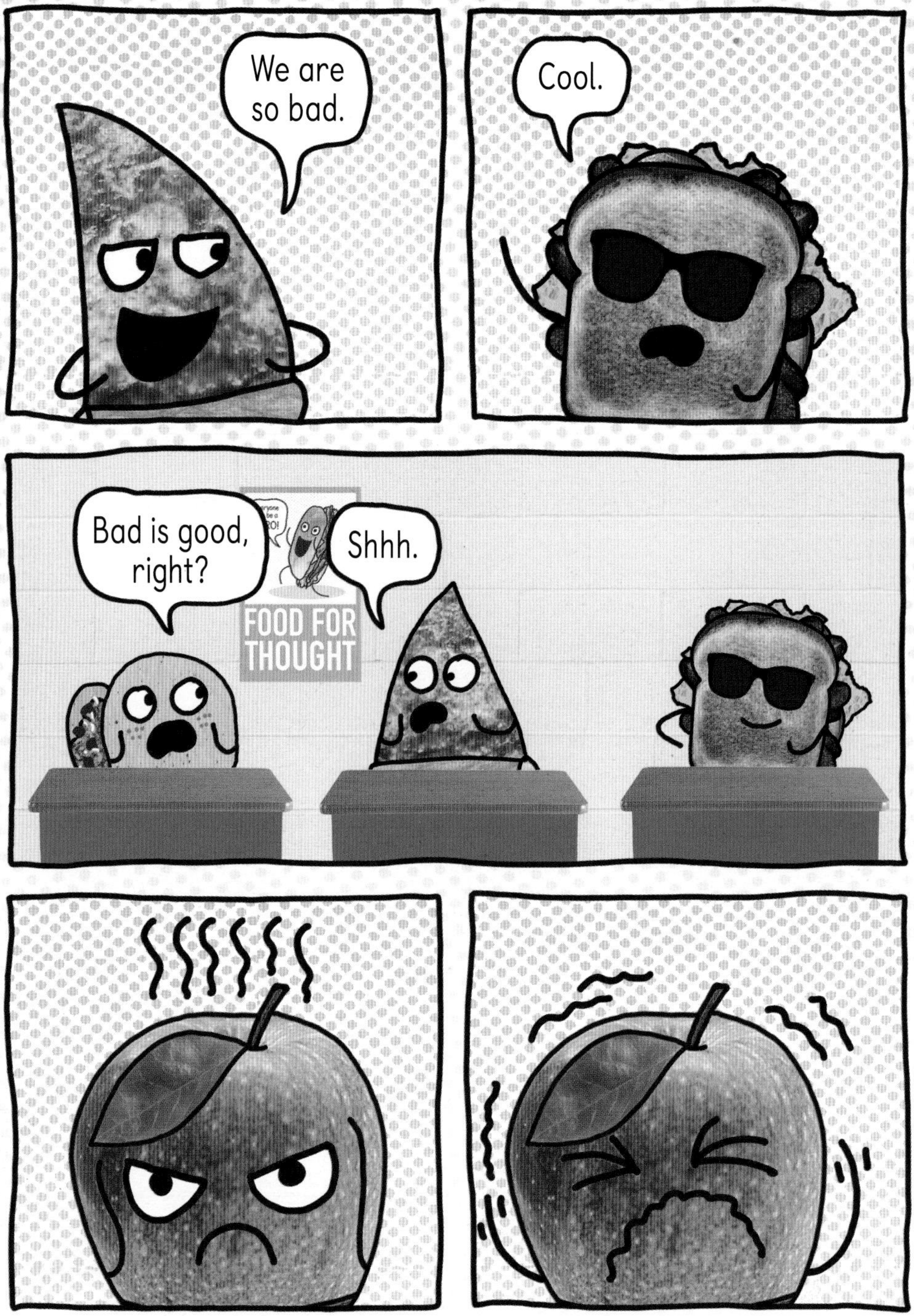
We are so bad.
Cool.
Bad is good, right?
Shhh.
FOOD FOR THOUGHT

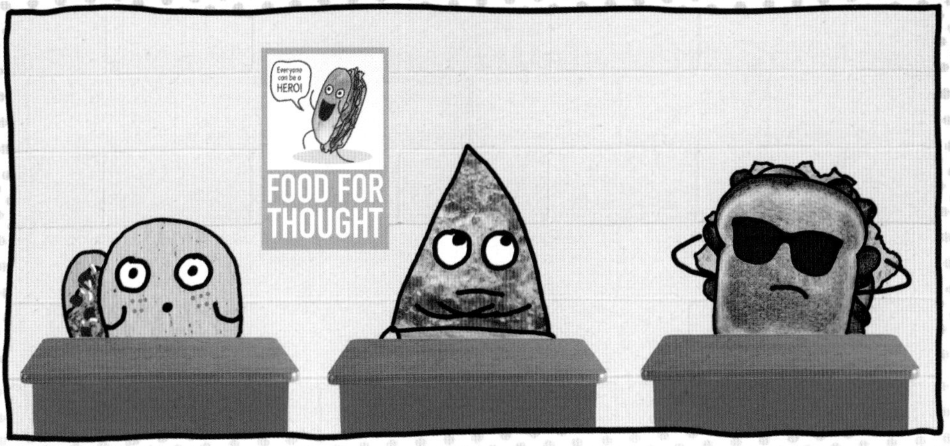
Everyone can be a HERO!
FOOD FOR THOUGHT

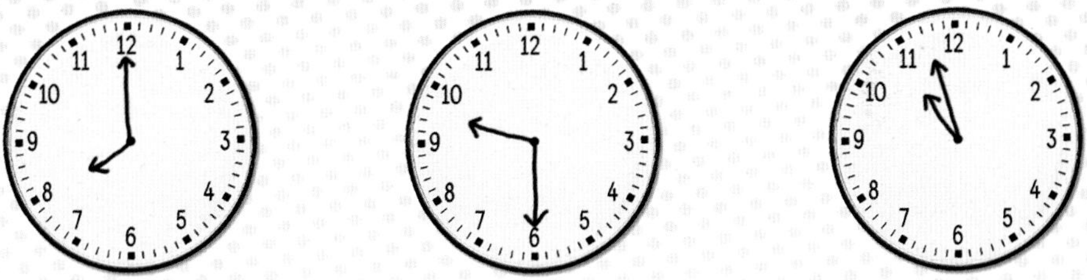

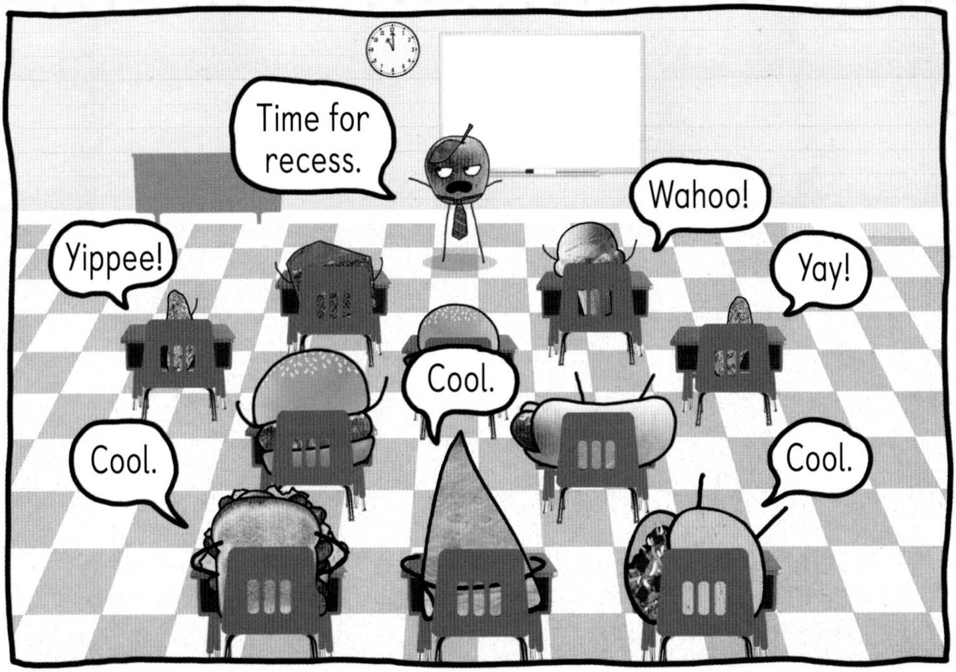
Time for recess.
Wahoo!
Yippee!
Yay!
Cool.
Cool.
Cool.

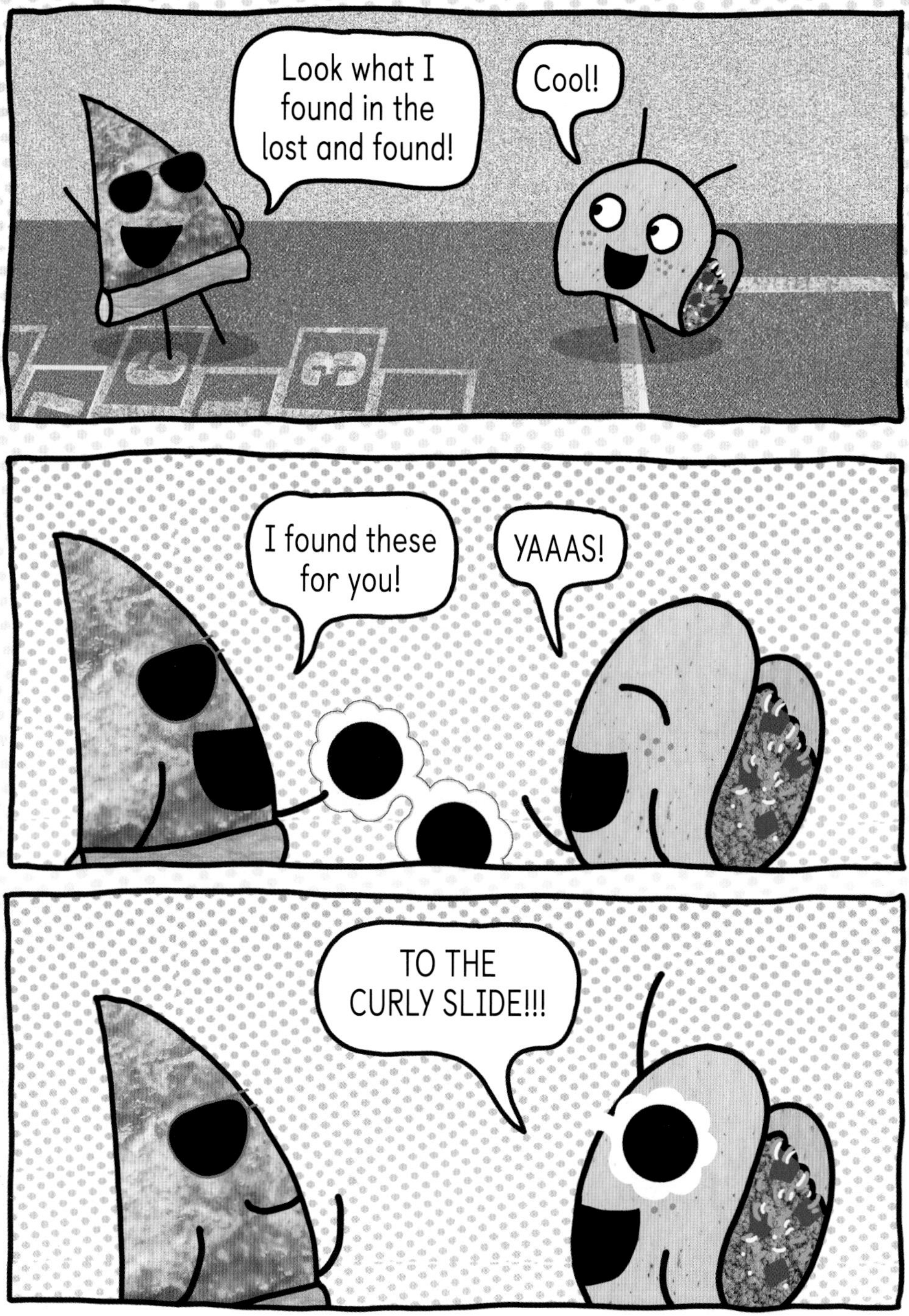
Look what I found in the lost and found!
Cool!
I found these for you!
YAAAS!
TO THE CURLY SLIDE!!!

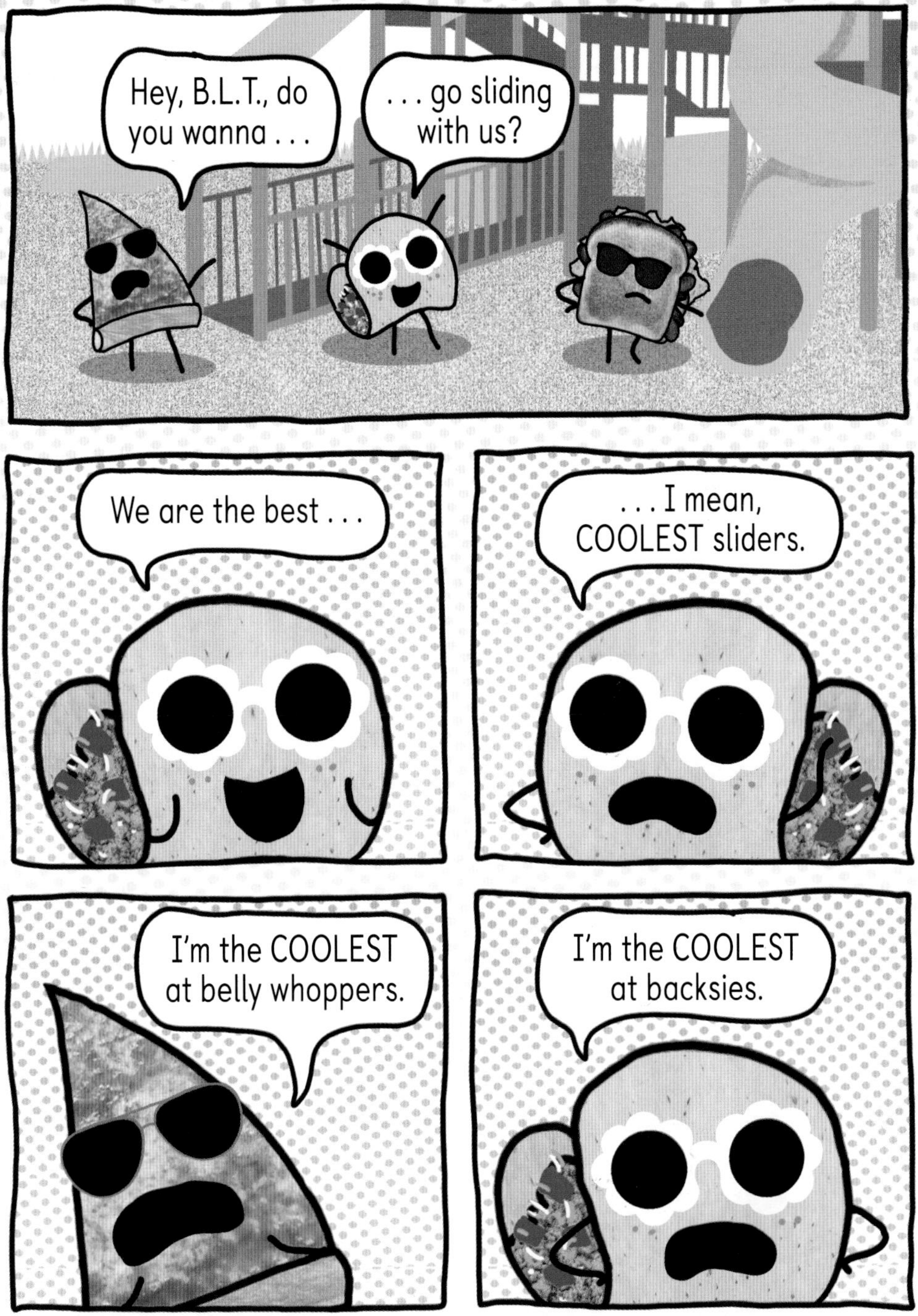
Hey, B.L.T., do you wanna . . .
. . . go sliding with us?
We are the best . . .
. . . I mean, COOLEST sliders.
I'm the COOLEST at belly whoppers.
I'm the COOLEST at backsies.

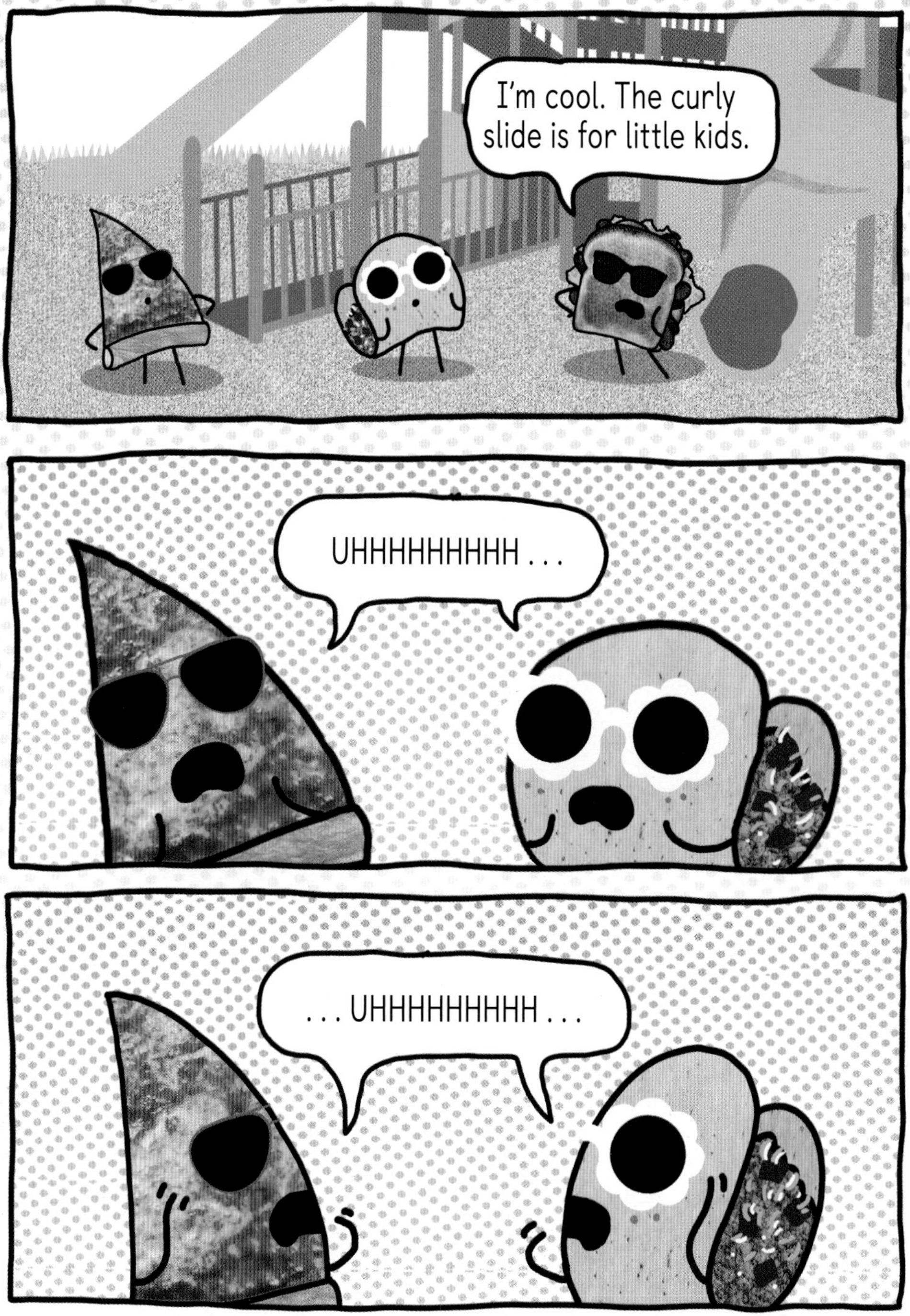
I'm cool. The curly slide is for little kids.
UHHHHHHHHH . . .
. . . UHHHHHHHHH . . .

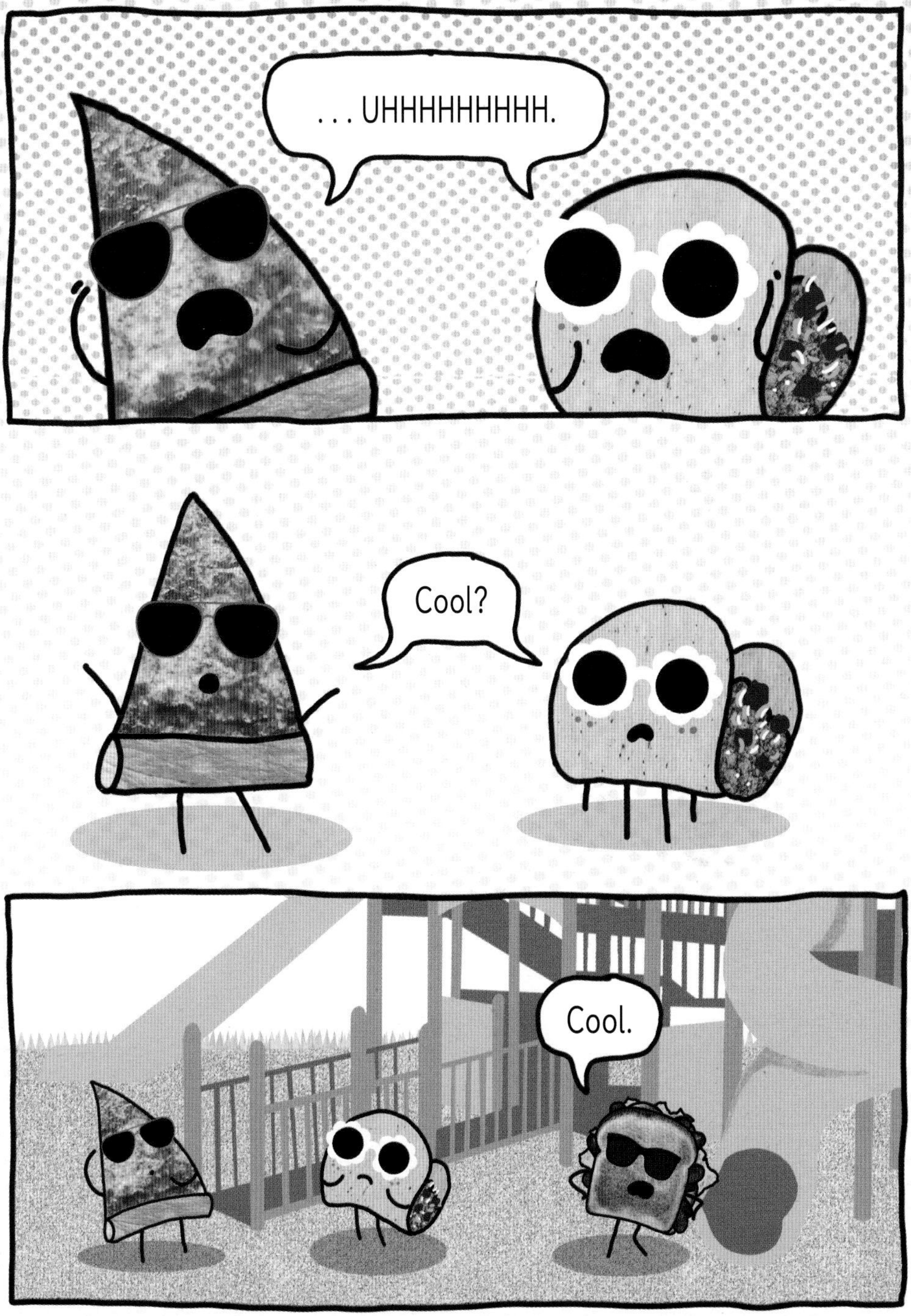
. . . UHHHHHHHHH.
Cool?
Cool.

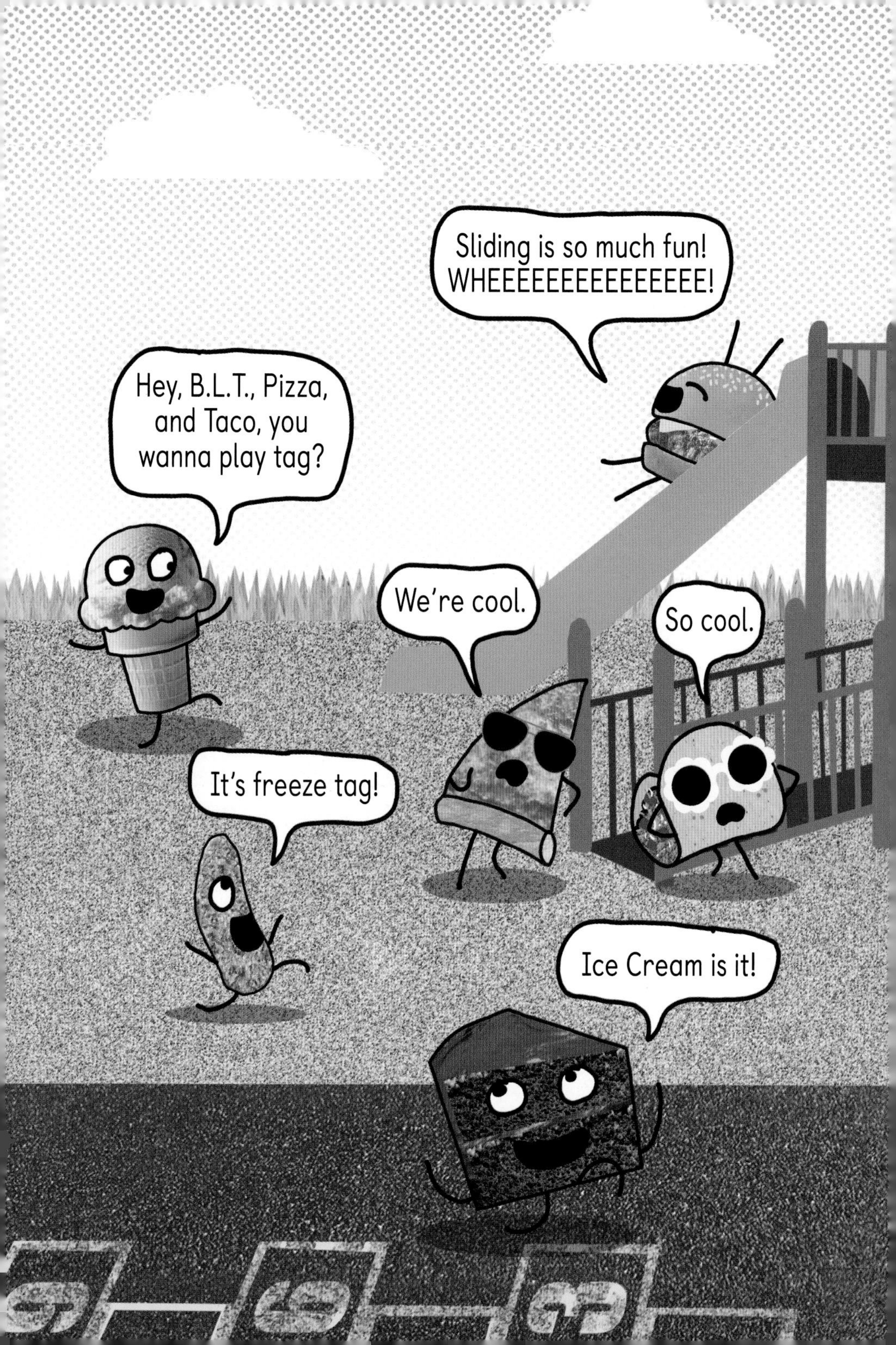
Sliding is so much fun! WHEEEEEEEEEEEEEEEE!
Hey, B.L.T., Pizza, and Taco, you wanna play tag?
We're cool.
So cool.
It's freeze tag!
Ice Cream is it!

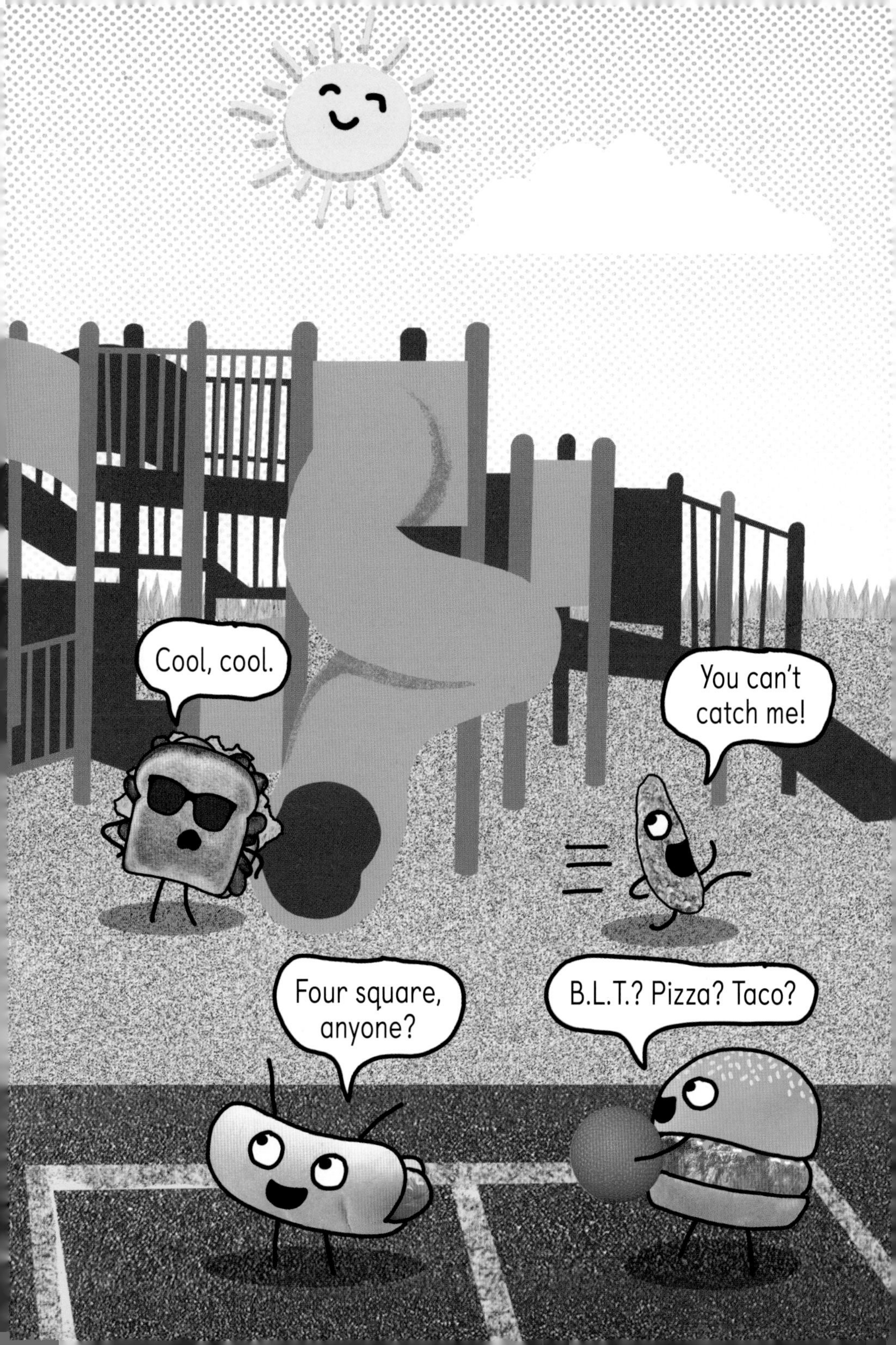
Cool, cool.
You can't catch me!
Four square, anyone?
B.L.T.? Pizza? Taco?

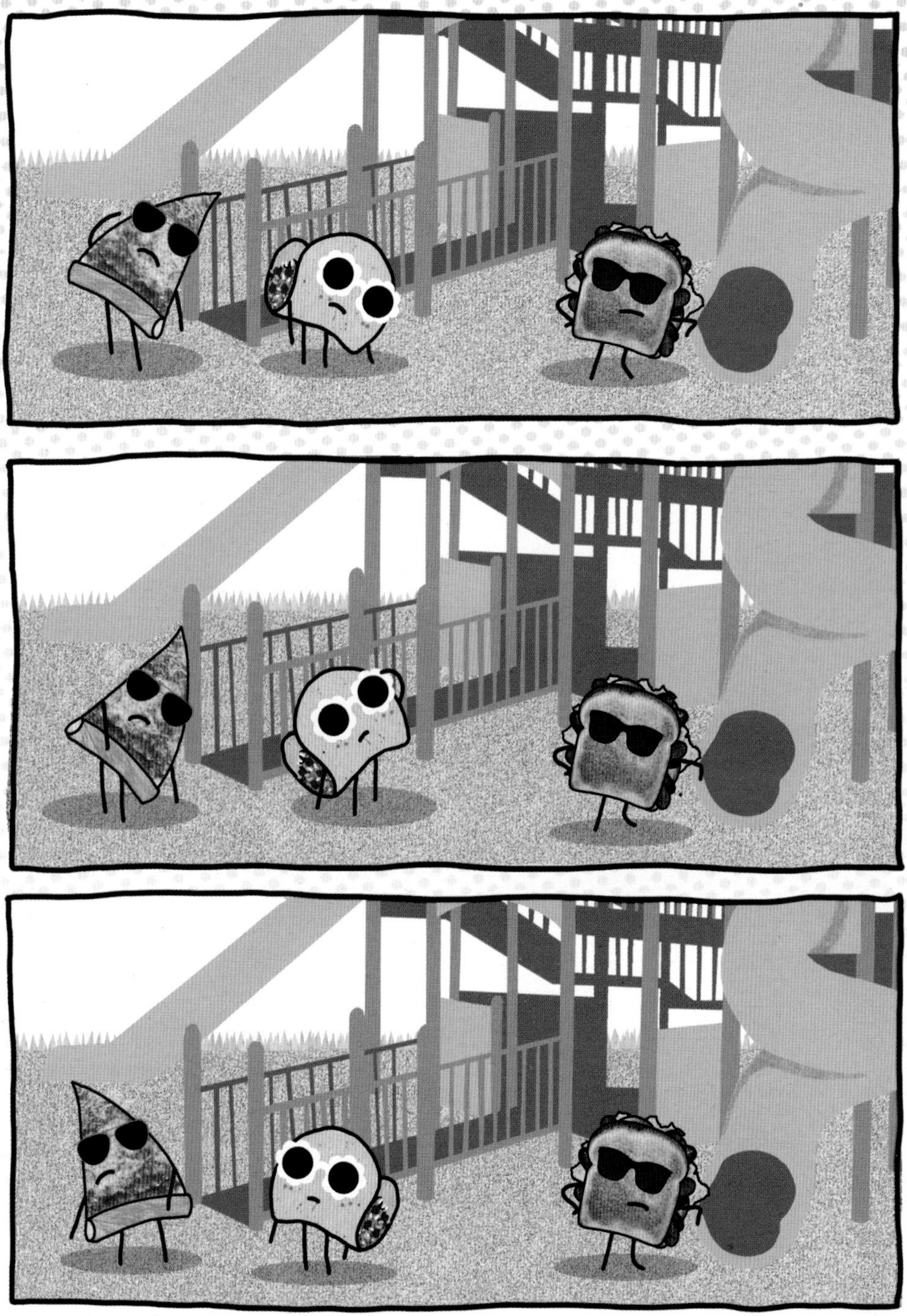

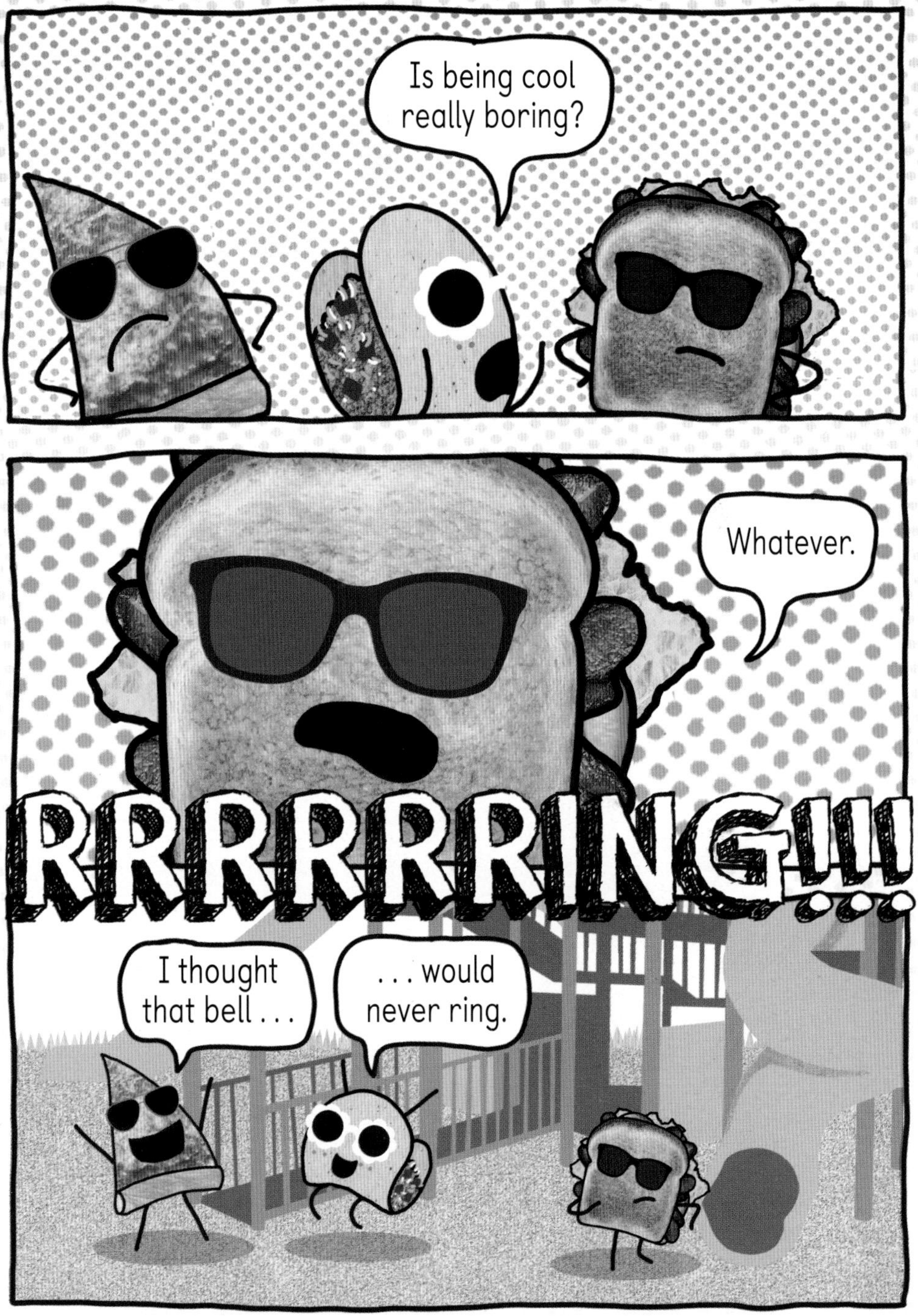
Is being cool really boring?
Whatever.
RRRRRRRING!!!
I thought that bell . . .
. . . would never ring.

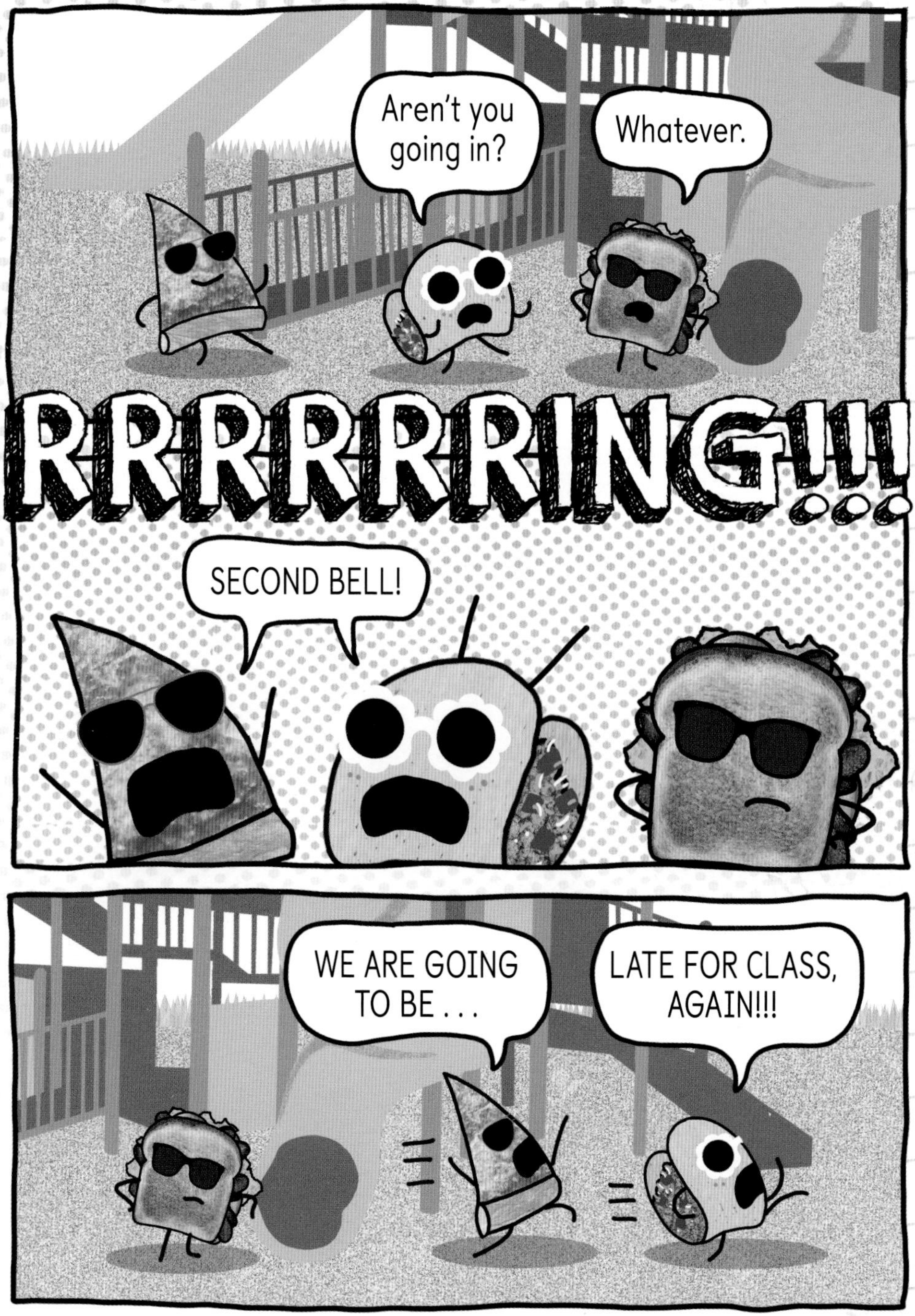
Aren't you going in?
Whatever.
RRRRRRRING!!!
SECOND BELL!
WE ARE GOING TO BE . . .
LATE FOR CLASS, AGAIN!!!

Chapter 4
Late for Class, Again

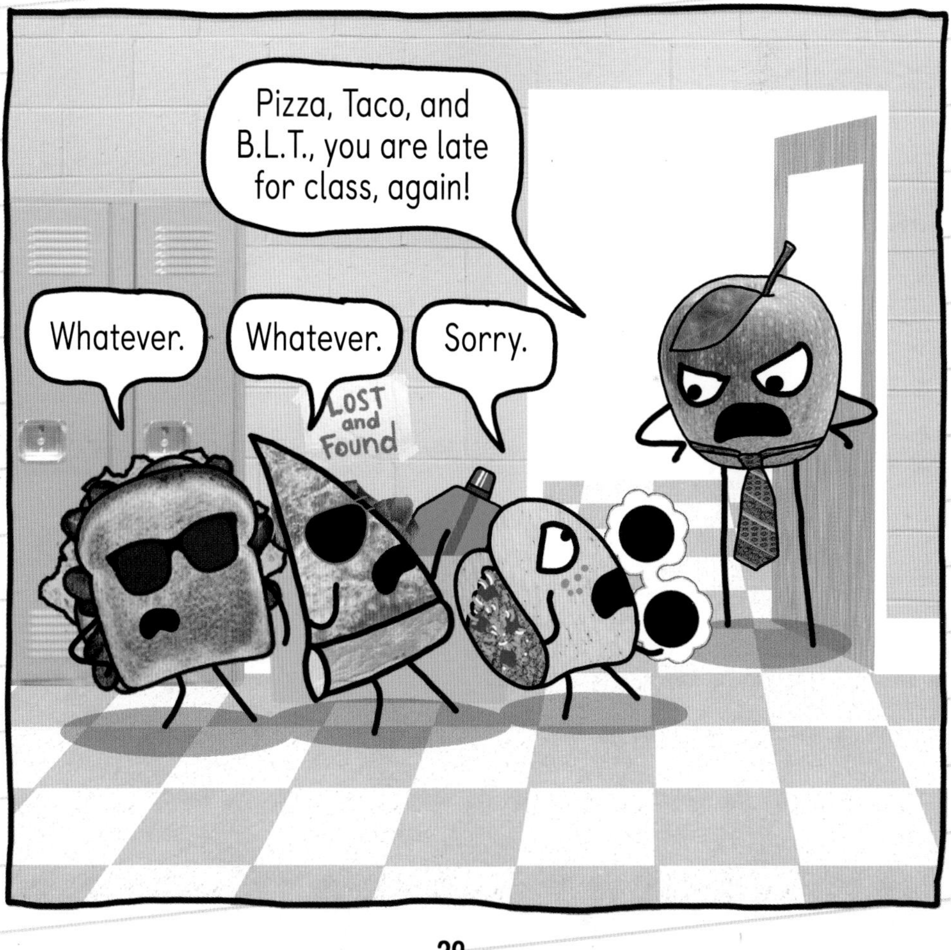
Pizza, Taco, and B.L.T., you are late for class, again!
Whatever.
Whatever.
Sorry.
LOST and Found

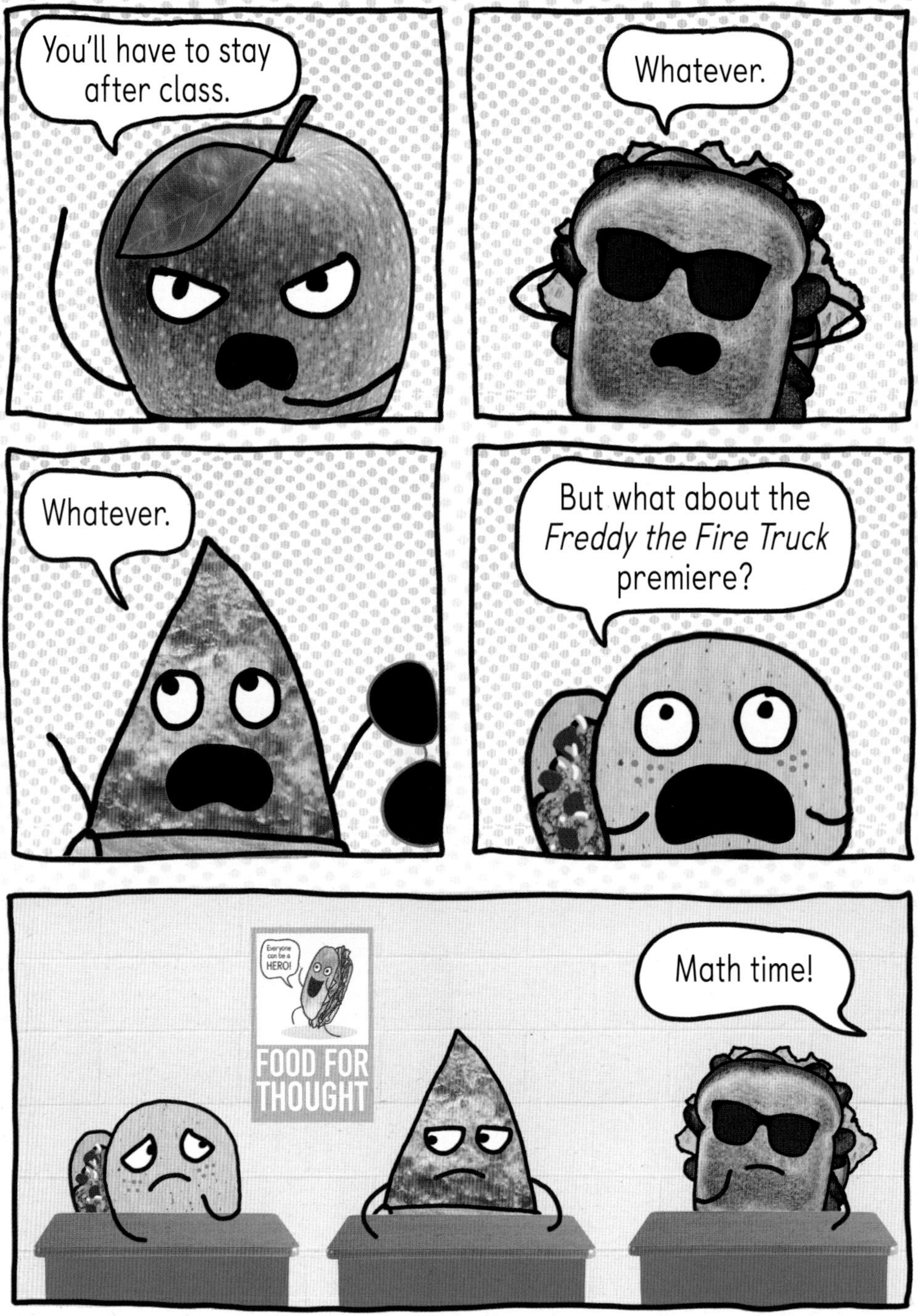
You'll have to stay after class.
Whatever.
Whatever.
But what about the *Freddy the Fire Truck* premiere?
Everyone can be a HERO!
FOOD FOR THOUGHT
Math time!

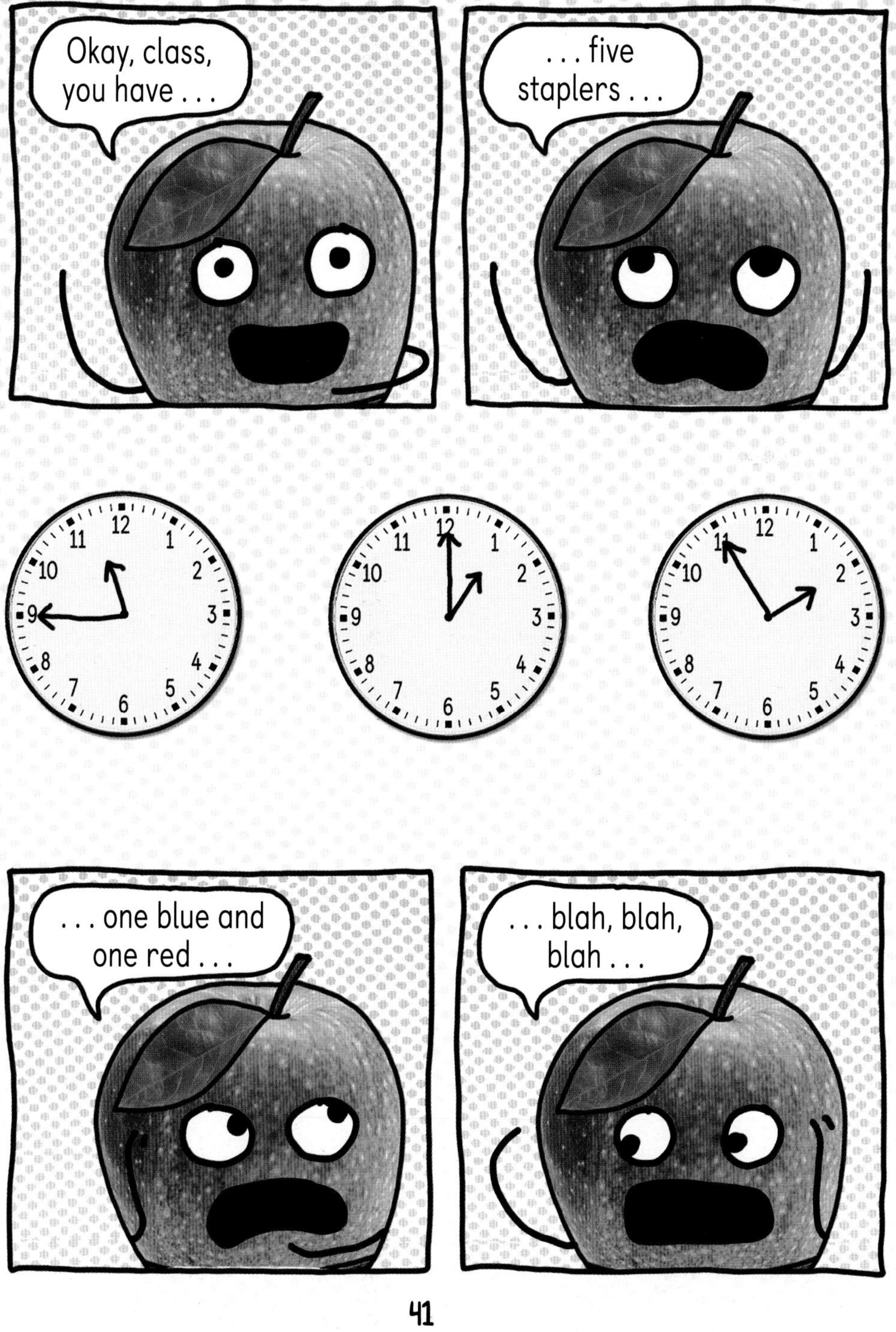
Okay, class, you have . . .
. . . five staplers . . .
. . . one blue and one red . . .
. . . blah, blah, blah . . .

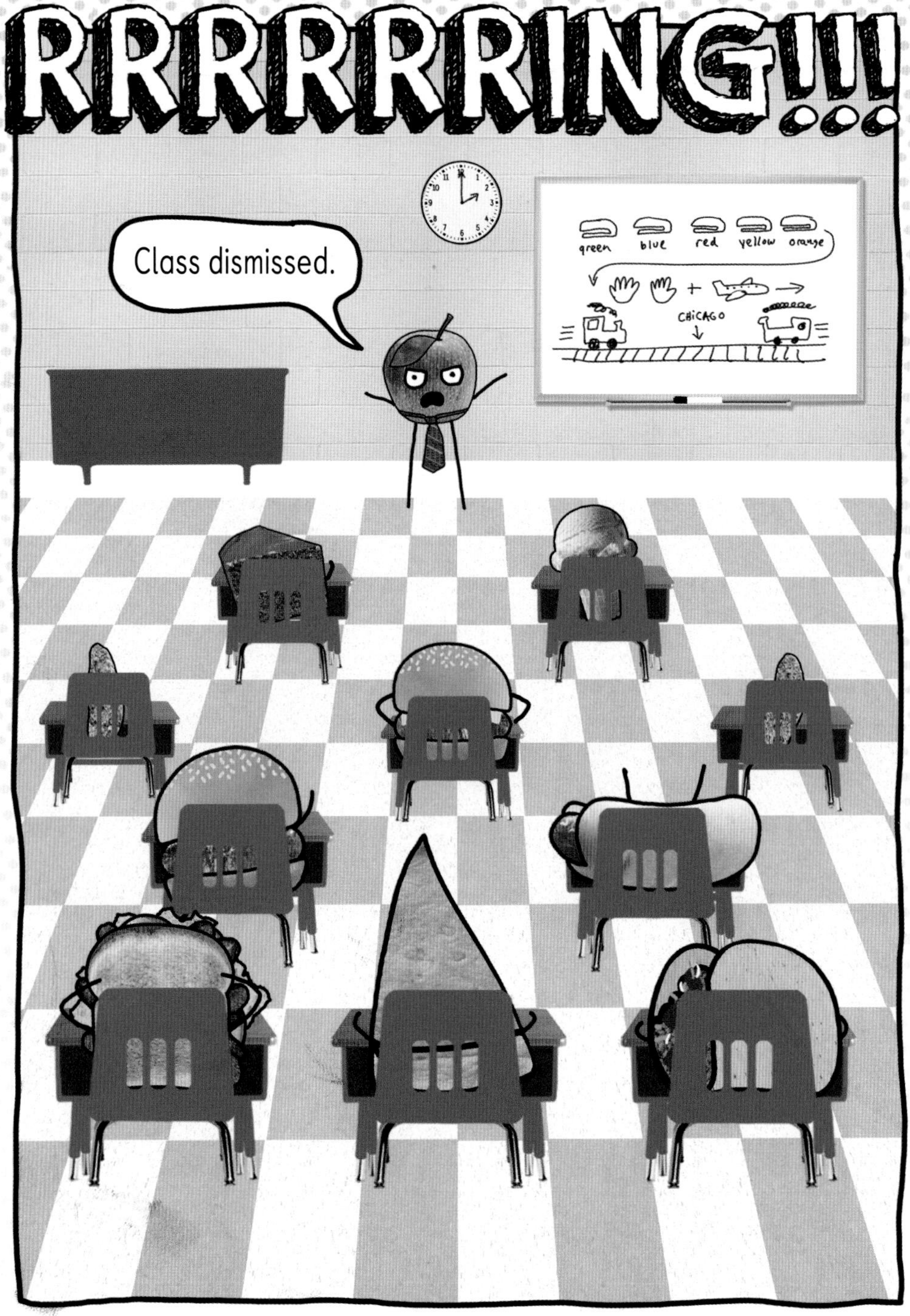
RRRRRRRING!!!
Class dismissed.
green blue red yellow orange
CHICAGO

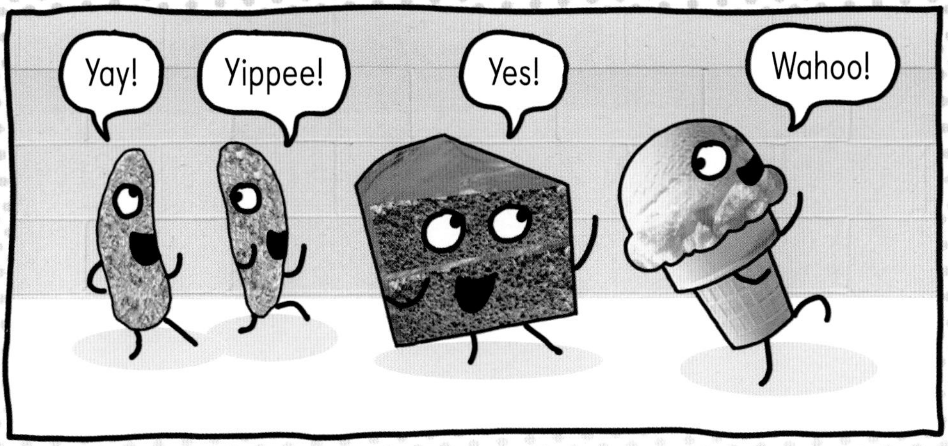
Yay!
Yippee!
Yes!
Wahoo!

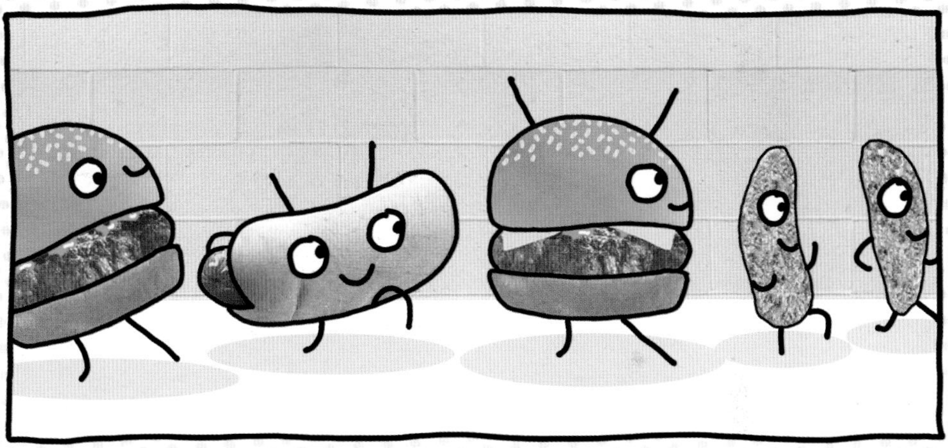

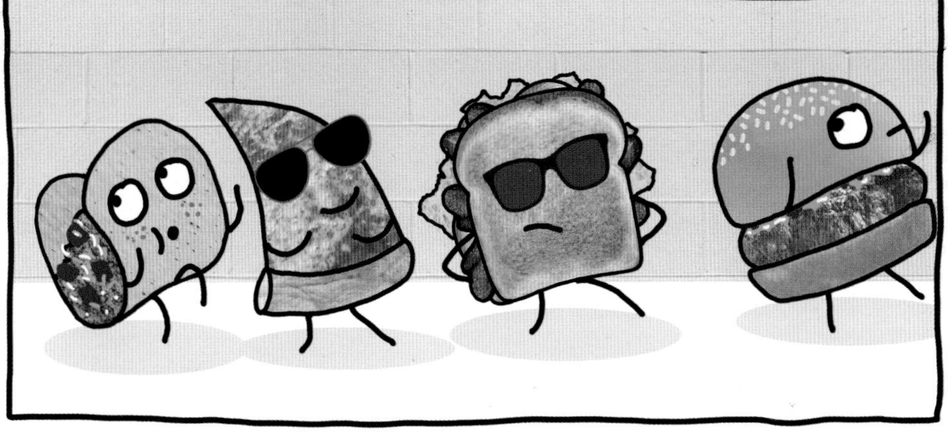

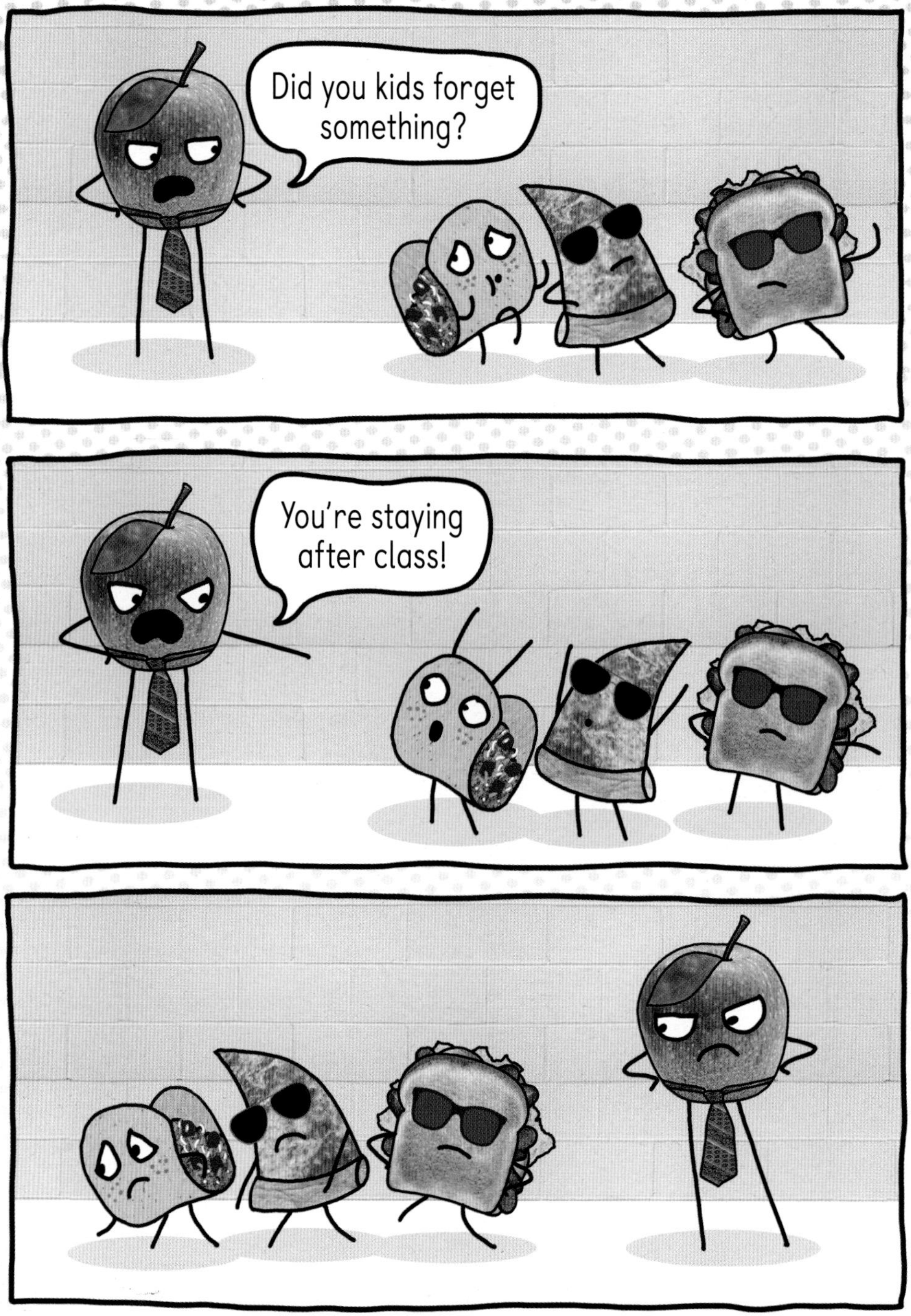
Did you kids forget something?
You're staying after class!

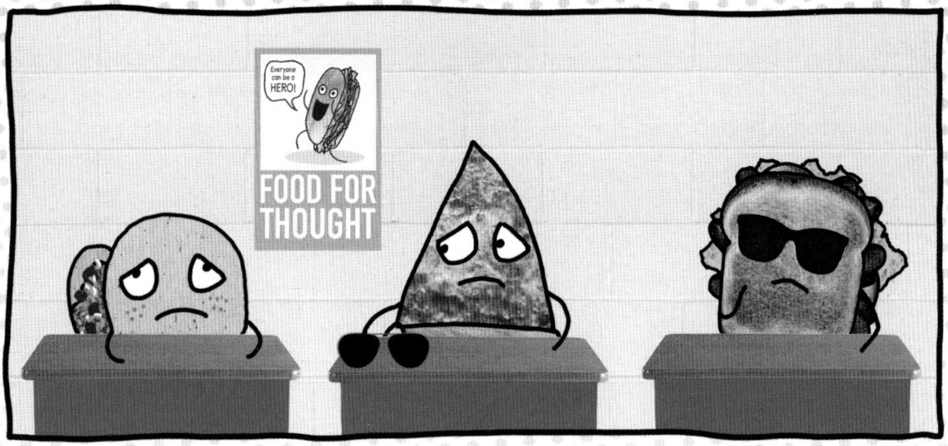
Everyone can be a HERO!
FOOD FOR THOUGHT

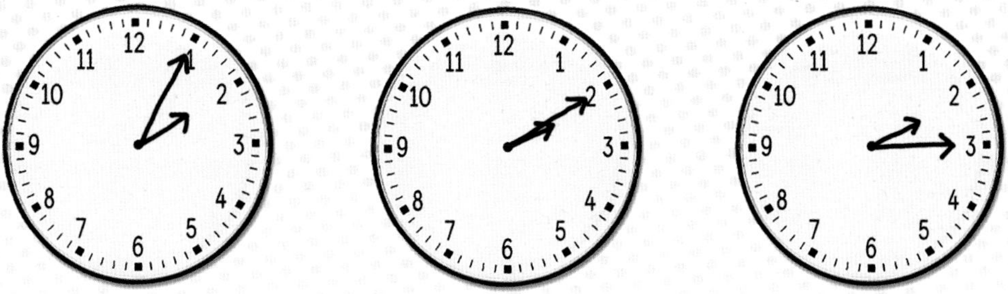

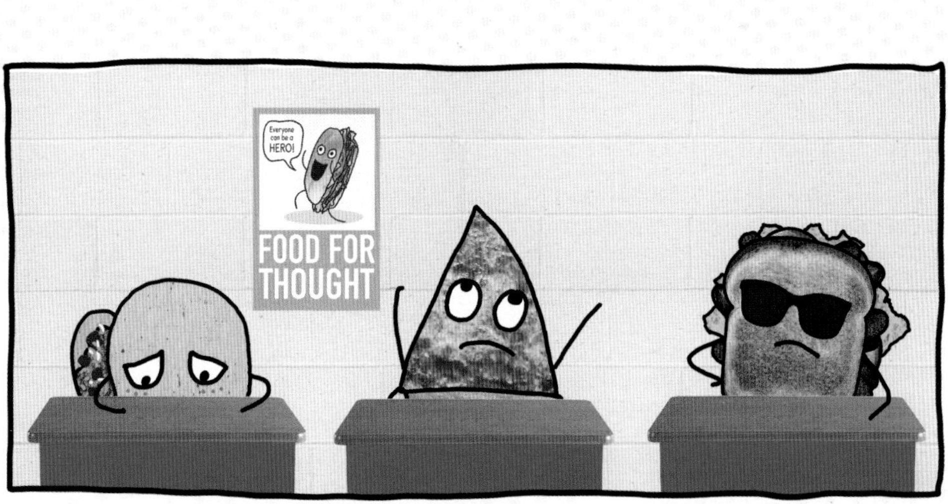
Everyone can be a HERO!
FOOD FOR THOUGHT

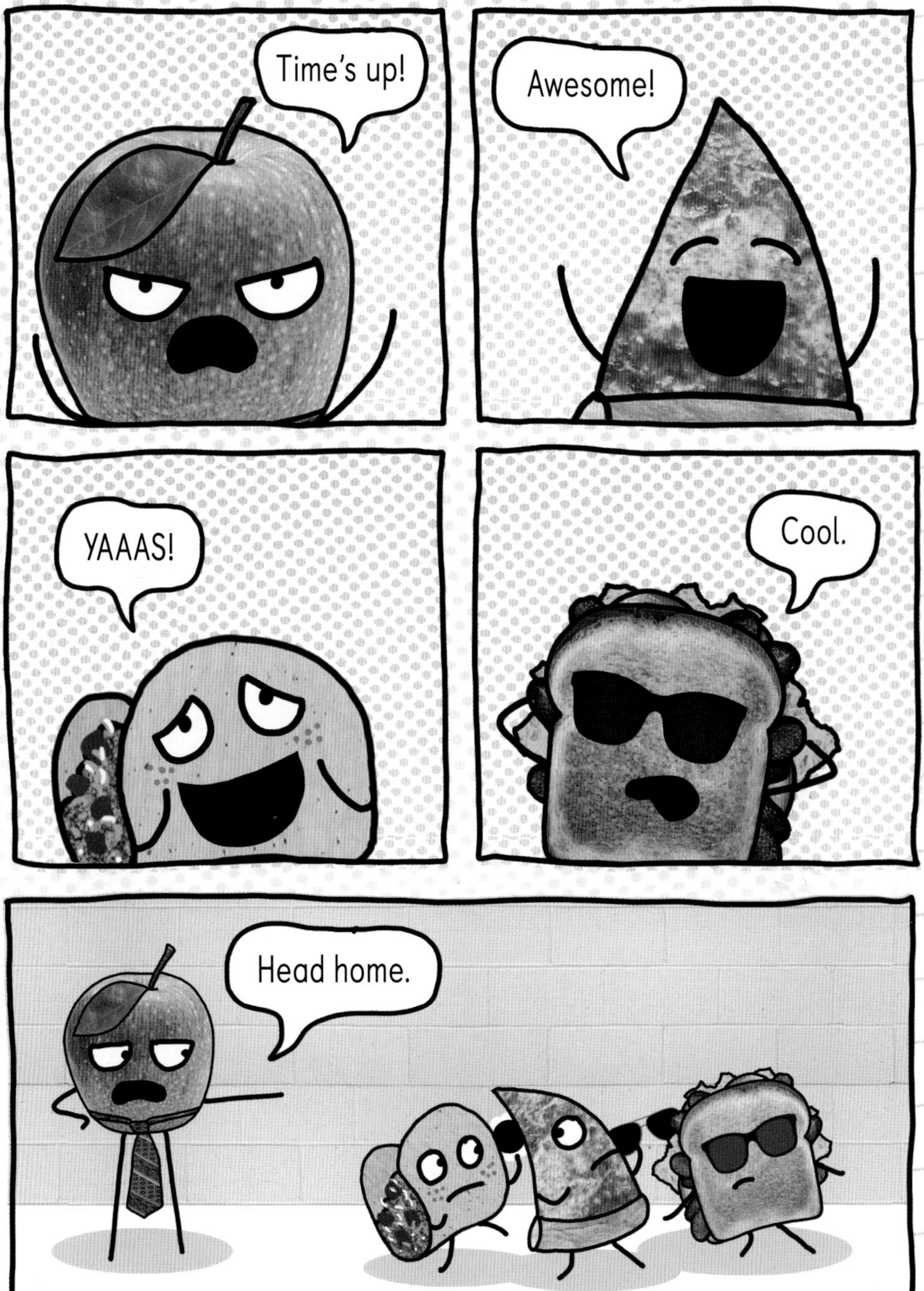
Time's up!
Awesome!
YAAAS!
Cool.
Head home.

Chapter 5
Pizza and Taco Head Home

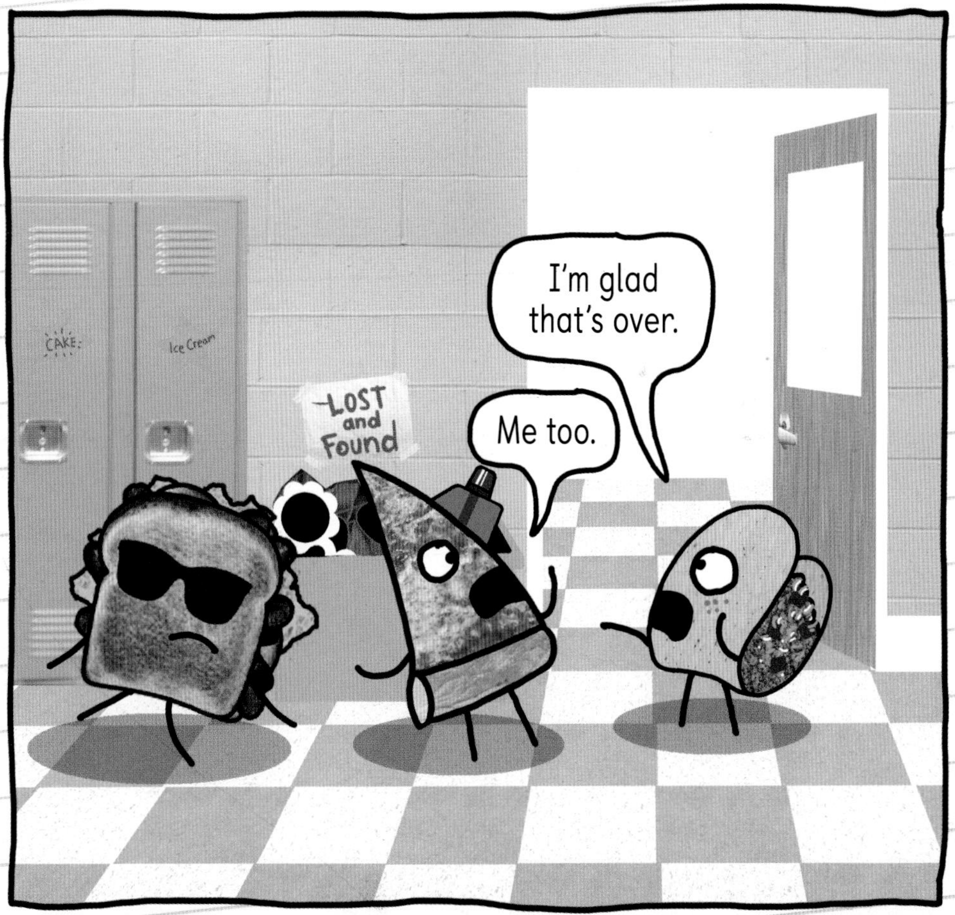

CAKE
Ice Cream
LOST and Found
I'm glad that's over.
Me too.

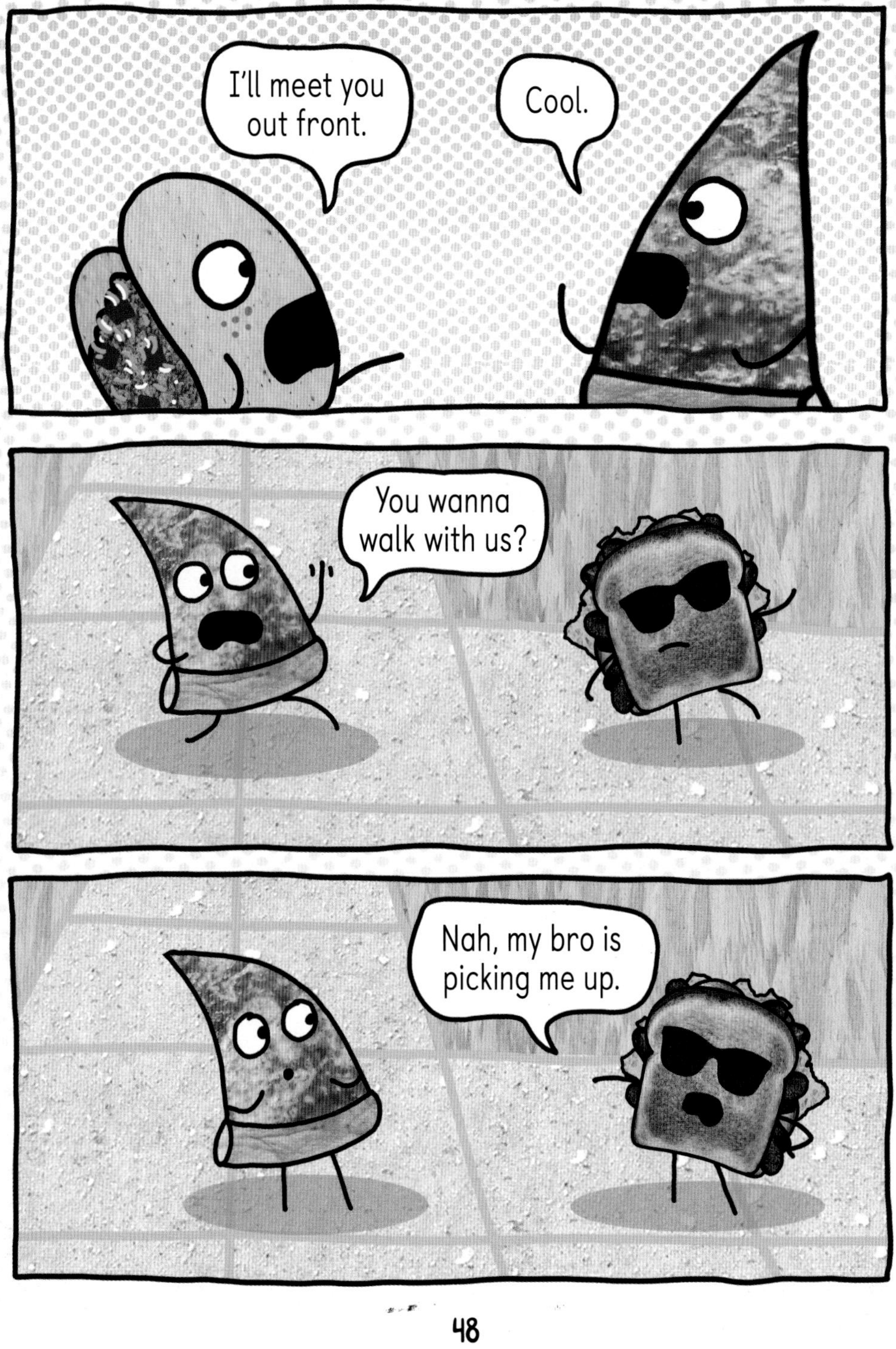
I'll meet you out front.
Cool.
You wanna walk with us?
Nah, my bro is picking me up.

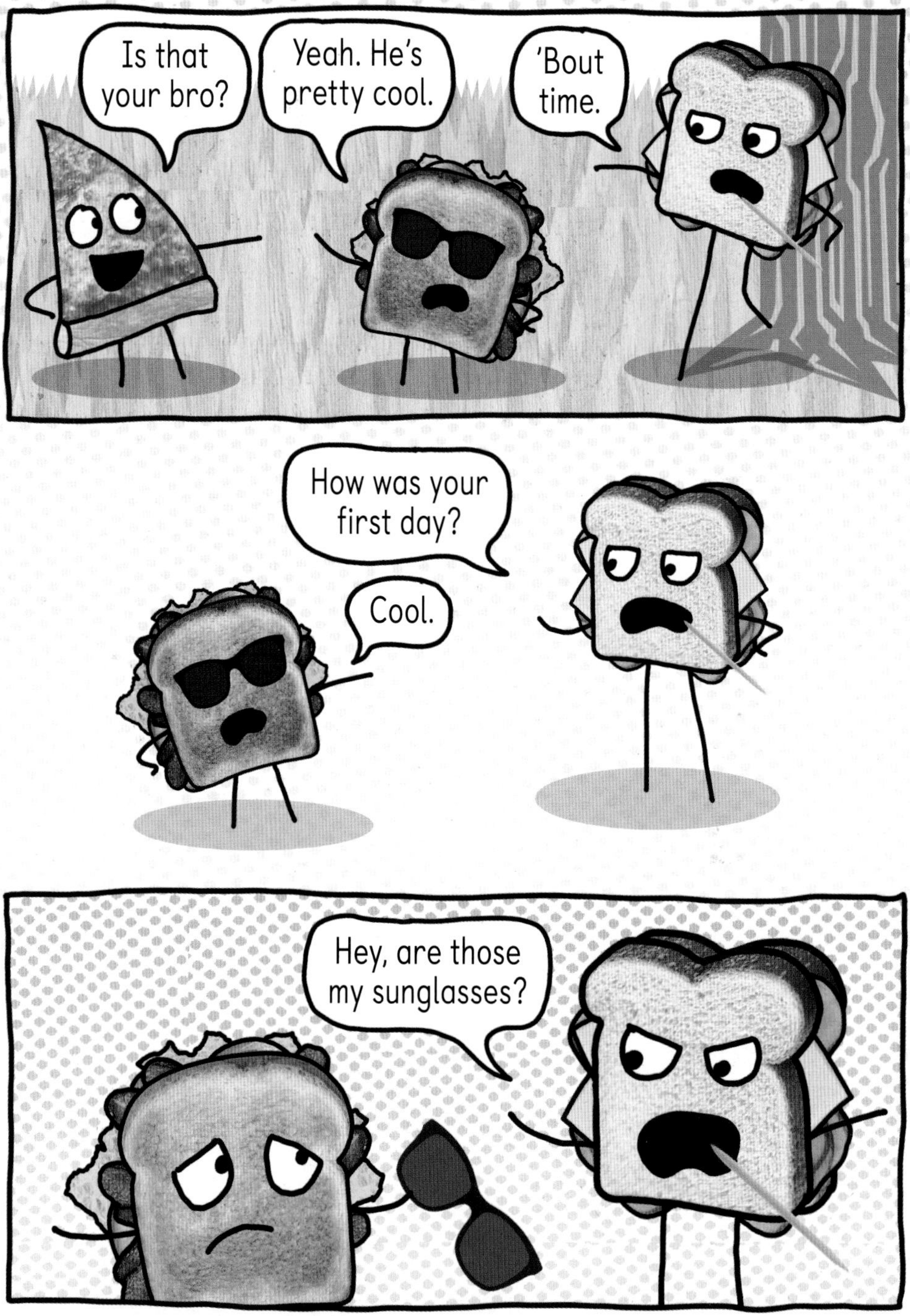
Is that your bro?
Yeah. He's pretty cool.
'Bout time.
How was your first day?
Cool.
Hey, are those my sunglasses?

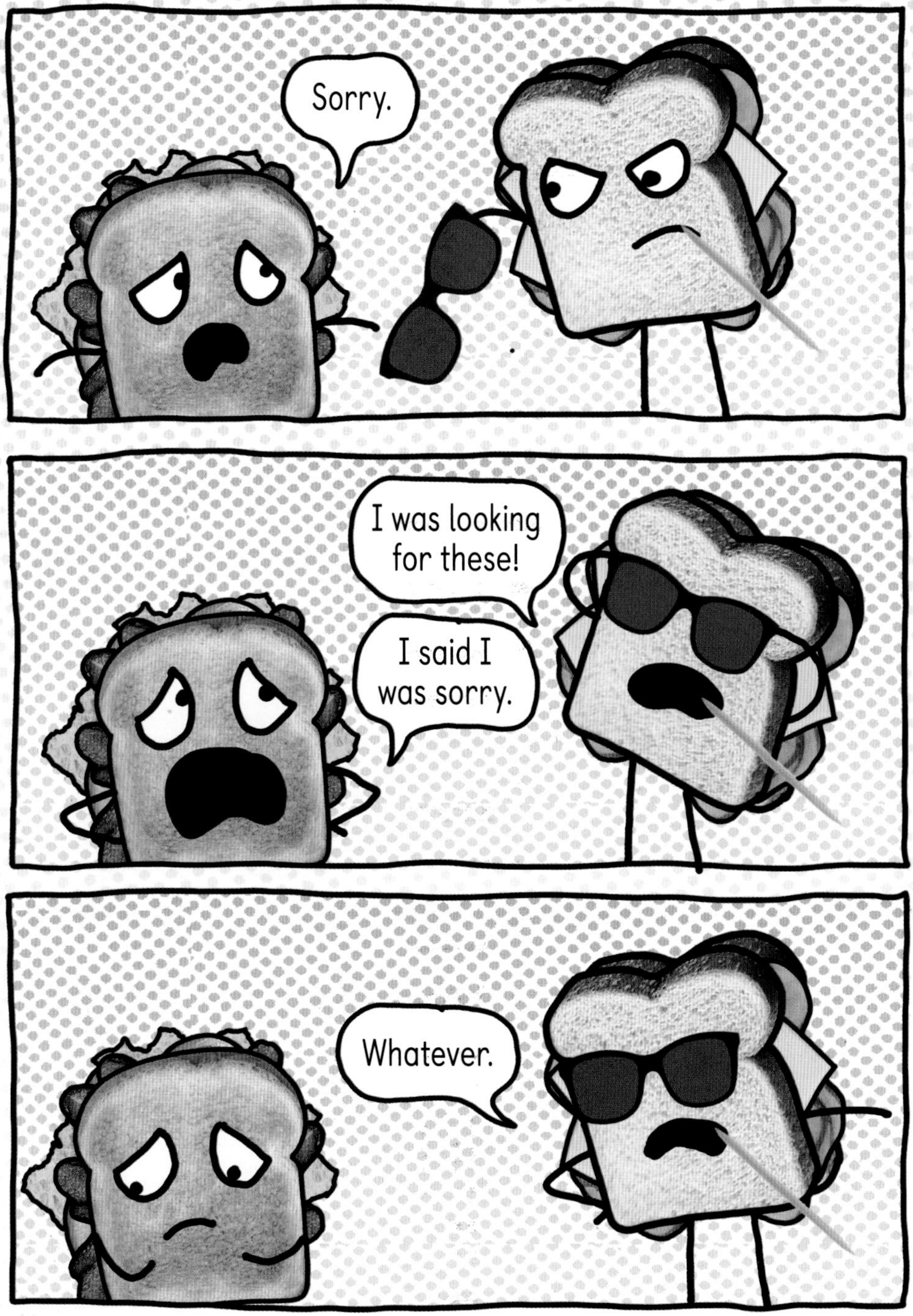
Sorry.
I was looking for these!
I said I was sorry.
Whatever.

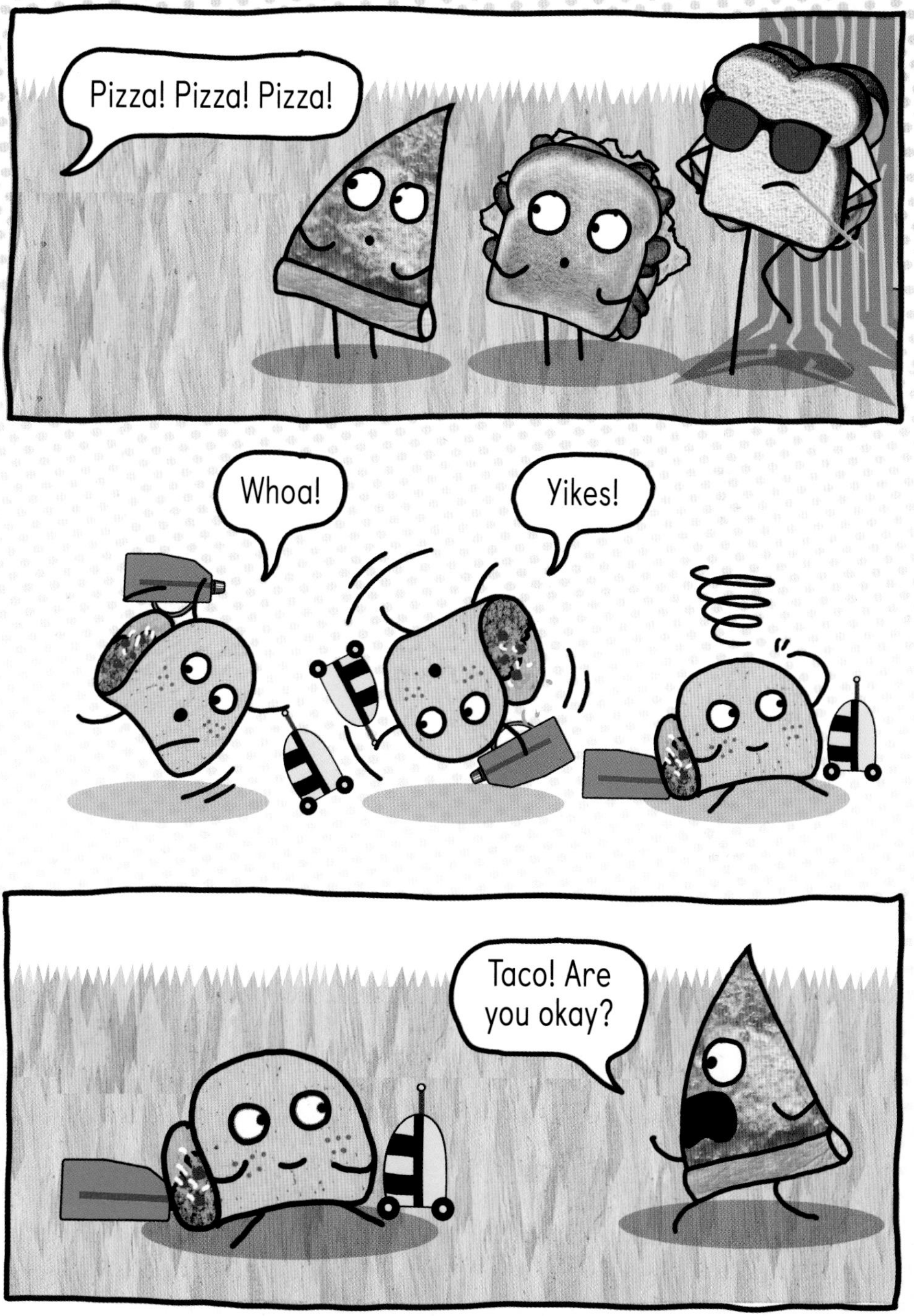
Pizza! Pizza! Pizza!
Whoa!
Yikes!
Taco! Are you okay?

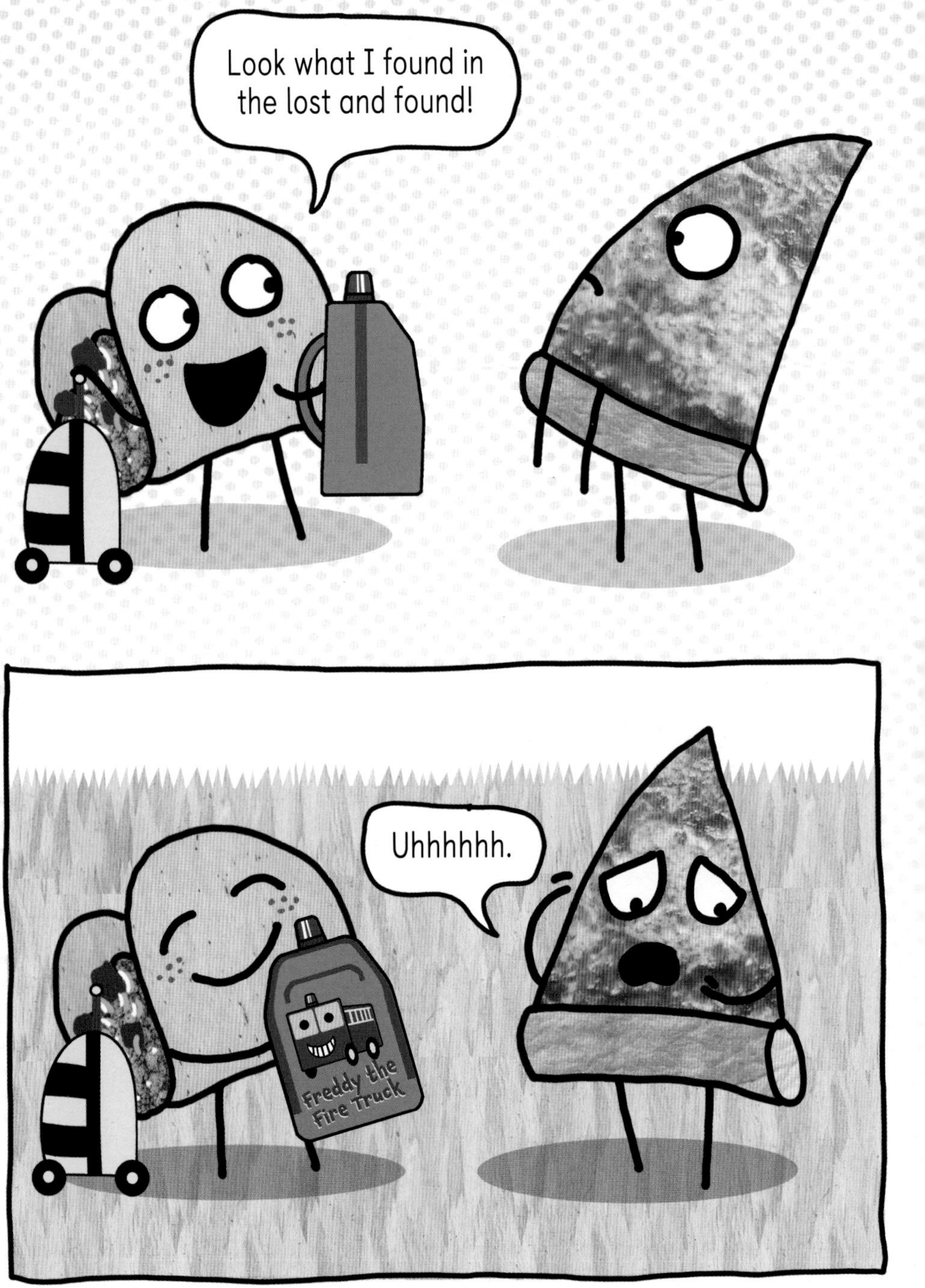
Look what I found in the lost and found!
Uhhhhhh.
Freddy the Fire Truck

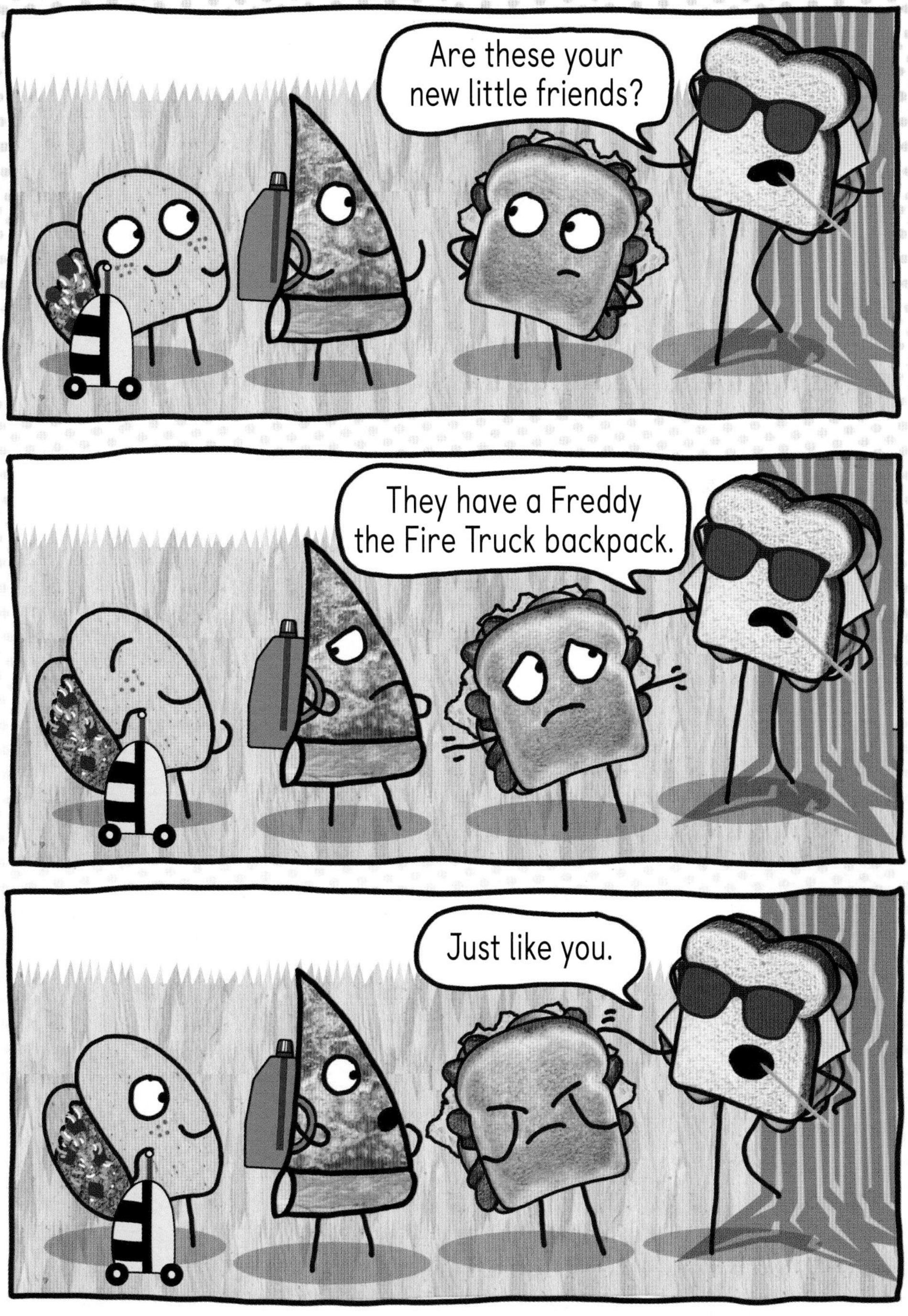
Are these your new little friends?
They have a Freddy the Fire Truck backpack.
Just like you.

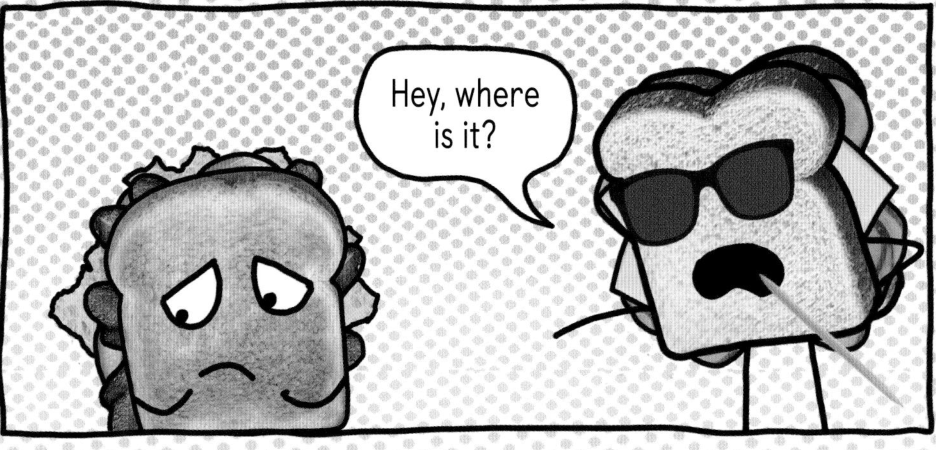
Hey, where is it?

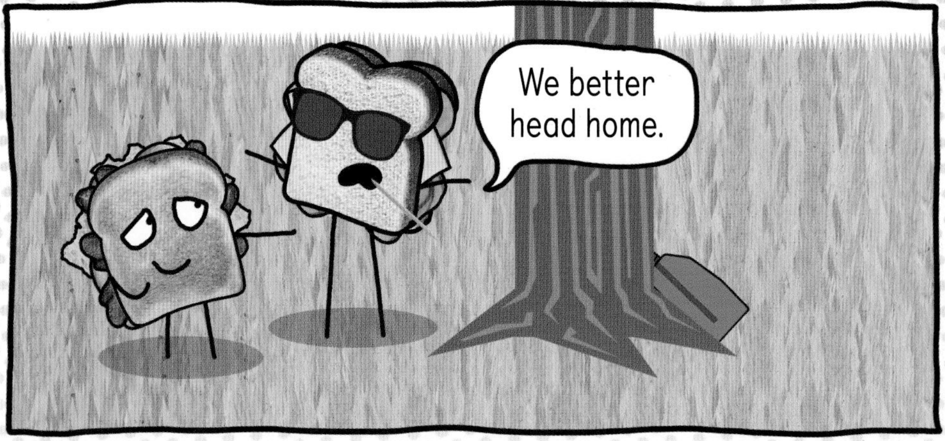
We better head home.

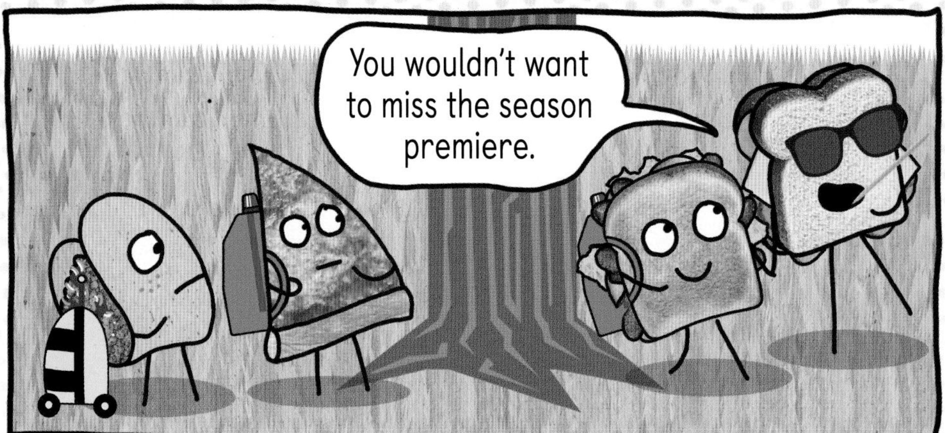
You wouldn't want to miss the season premiere.

Bye.

See you tomorrow.

Bye!

We should head home too!

Sound the Super Siren!

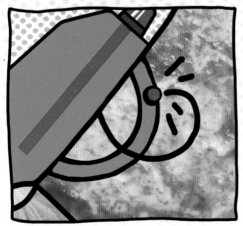

SUPER SIREN!

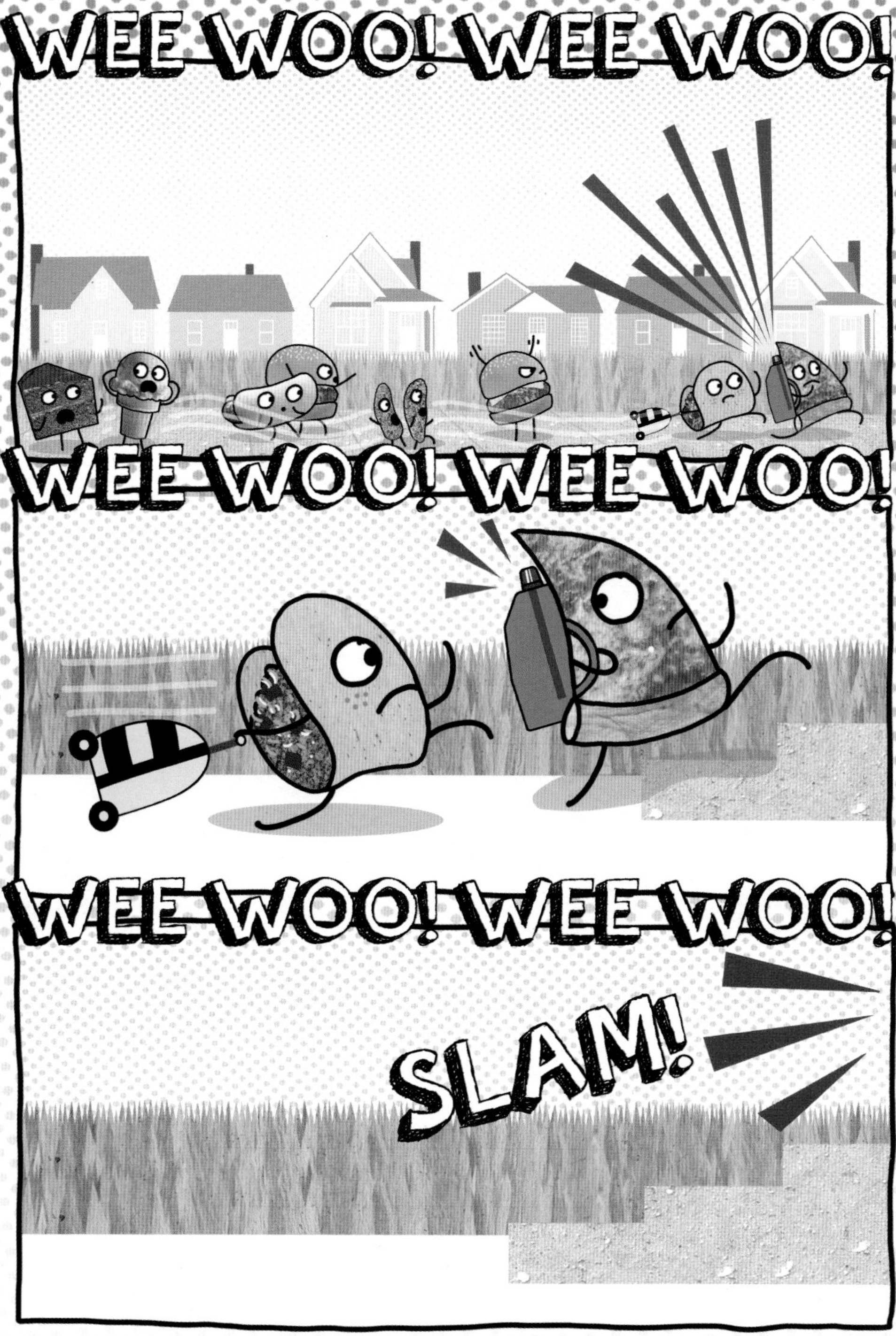
WEE WOO! WEE WOO!
WEE WOO! WEE WOO!
WEE WOO! WEE WOO!
SLAM!

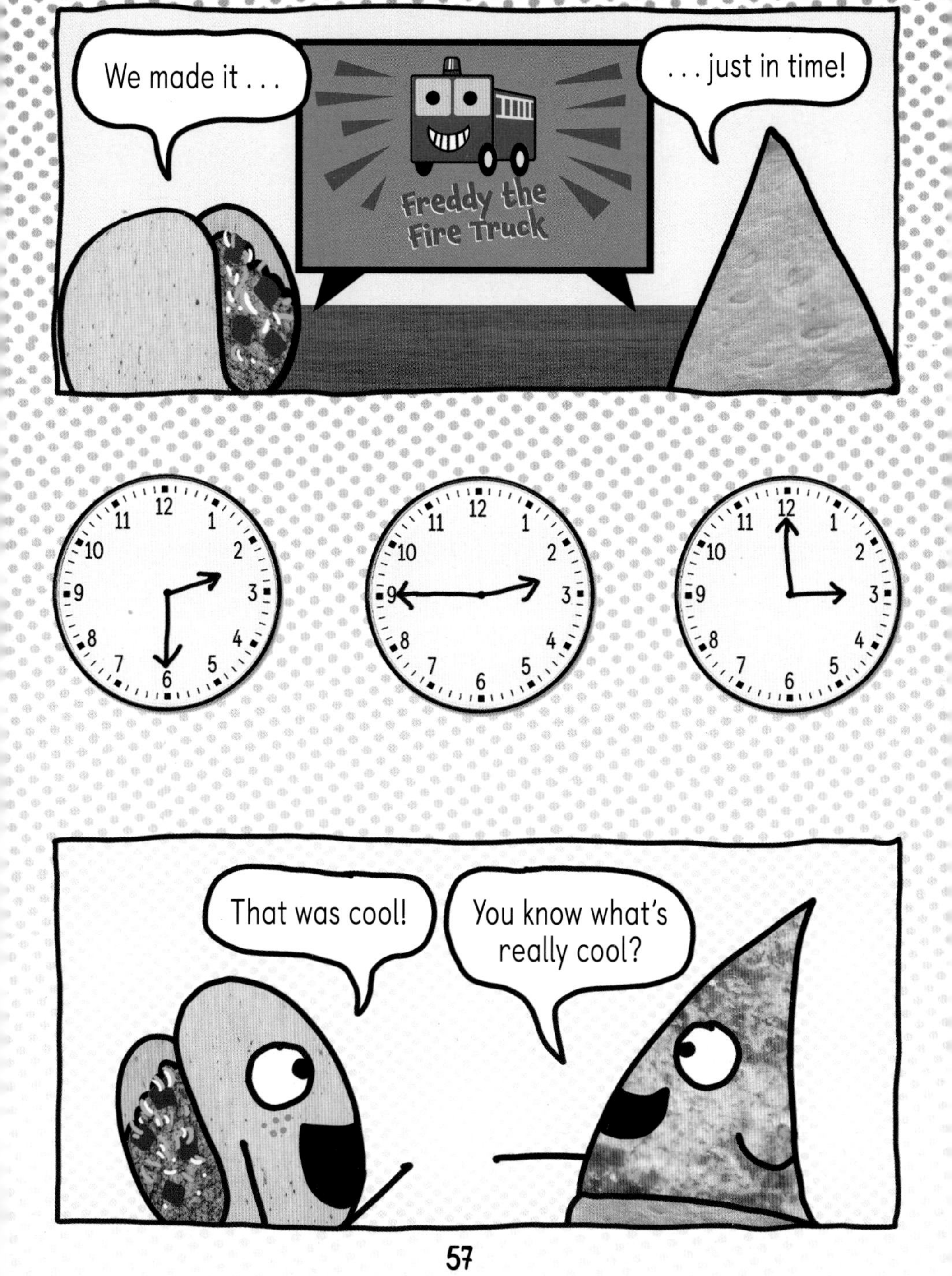
We made it . . .
Freddy the Fire Truck
. . . just in time!
That was cool!
You know what's really cool?

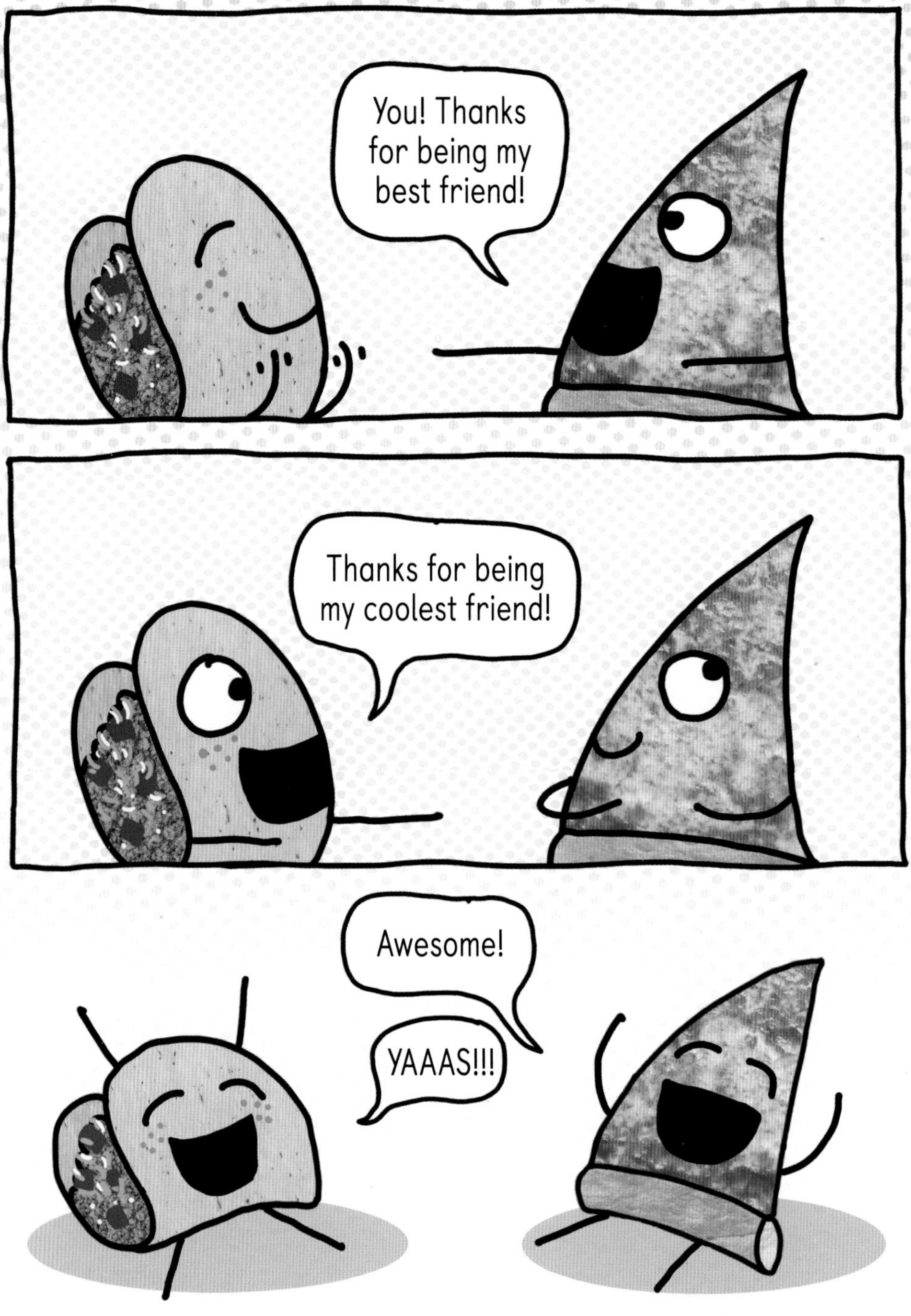
You! Thanks for being my best friend!
Thanks for being my coolest friend!
Awesome!
YAAAS!!!

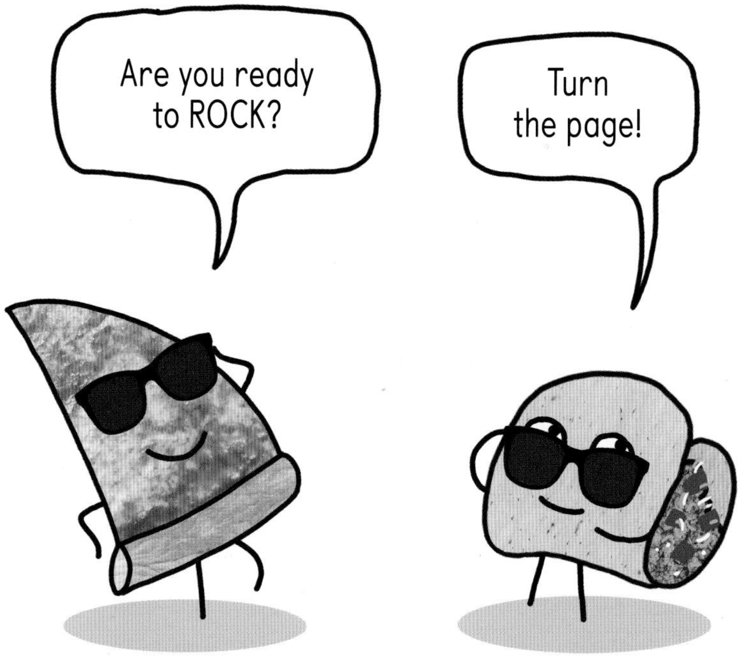
Are you ready to ROCK?
Turn the page!

Could Pizza and Taco get any cooler?

HOW TO BE A BAND

1. Make up a cool band name.
2. Choose a sound.
3. Get instruments.
4. Learn to play.
5. Write songs.

How hard can it be?
Let's start a band!

PIZZA AND TACO: ROCK OUT!

Coming in January 2023!

SNEAK PEEK!
We need a name that is AWESOME!
YAAAS!

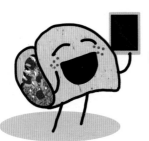

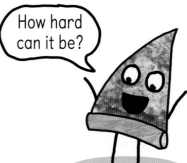

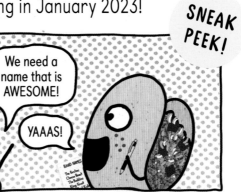

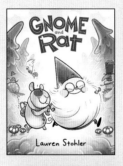

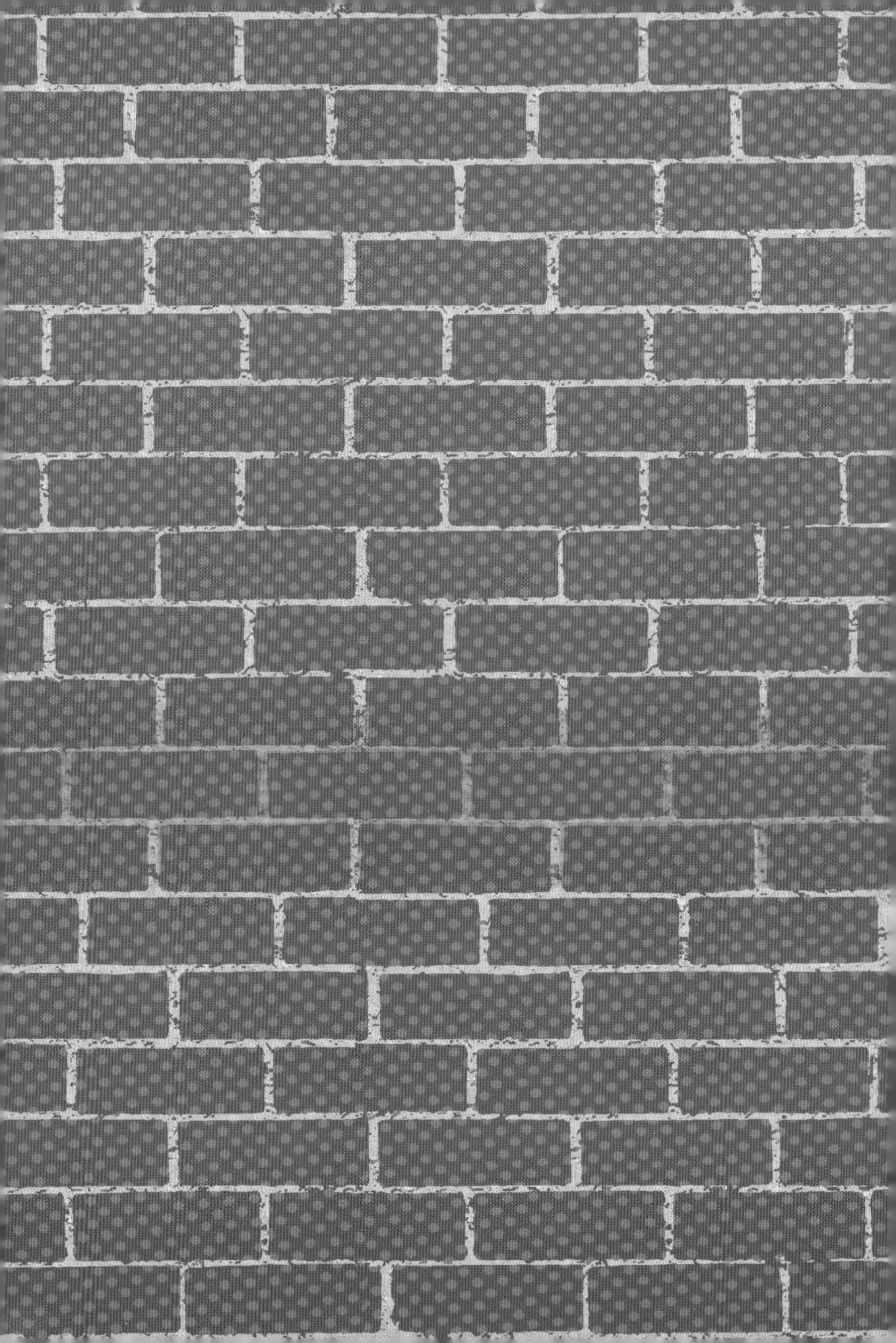